D0668501

STORIES FOR
9 YEAR OLDS

A Random House book
Published by Random House Australia Pty Ltd
Level 3, 100 Pacific Highway, North Sydney NSW 2060
www.randomhouse.com.au

First published by Random House Australia in 2014

Addresses for companies within the Random House Group can be found at
www.randomhouse.com.au/offices

National Library of Australia
Cataloguing-in-Publication Entry

Title: Stories for nine year olds/edited by Linsay Knight
ISBN: 978 0 85798 477 7 (pbk)
Target audience: For primary school age.
Subject: Children's stories, Australian.
Other authors/contributors:
    Knight, Linsay, editor
    Jellett, Tom, illustrator
Dewey number: A823.01089282

Cover illustration by Tom Jellett
Cover design by Leanne Beattie
Internal design and typesetting by Midland Typesetters, Australia
Printed in Australia by Griffin Press, an accredited ISO AS/NZS 14001:2004
Environmental Management System printer

STORIES FOR 9 YEAR OLDS

Stories by
JACQUELINE HARVEY, ANDY GRIFFITHS,
TRISTAN BANCKS AND MORE!

Edited by
LINSAY KNIGHT

Illustrated by
TOM JELLETT

RANDOM HOUSE AUSTRALIA

FOREWORD

BACK BY POPULAR DEMAND!

What a treat it is to search for the special stories that tickle childrens' tastebuds and find a treasured place on their burgeoning reading menus, to be sampled again and again. This collection showcases these stories in order to excite nine-year-old readers, enable them to test their growing skills and continue their reading adventure in a safe and reassuring environment. And that's why we have also given such careful consideration to the reading requirements of this age group, such as content, author style and voice, as well as the ratio of text to illustration and type size.

These independent readers can be encouraged to keep reading by tackling longer fiction (with the occasional illustrations) or interesting non-fiction (with cartoon-style illustrations). The exploration of other worlds through fantasy is a sign of a maturing outlook. The characters and events are important as well as the way in which they introduce readers to different ways of telling stories, as in third-person narrators. Stories at this level open a world of words to their readers, as well as to the many techniques writers use to tell their stories. As always, Tom Jellett's black-line illustrations add a layer of meaning to the text and interest to the reading experience.

The most advanced of four specially selected collections, *Stories for 9 Year Olds* includes offerings from the following inspirational Australian storytellers: Jacqueline Harvey, Tristan Bancks, Aleesah Darlison, Colin Thompson, Dianne Bates, George Ivanoff, Jenny Blackford, Kerri Lane, Michael Pryor and Andy Griffiths.

We are proud to present such a friendly and accessible book, essential for children who adore being read to and demand a good read.

— Linsay Knight

CONTENTS

ALICE-MIRANDA AND THE SECRETS OF SINTRA

BY JACQUELINE HARVEY

'Good morning, young ladies and gentleman,' the handsome manager of the restaurant greeted the children. 'May I offer you some juice?'

Alice-Miranda smiled at the man. 'Good morning, Mr Perreira. That would be lovely, thank you.'

'Yes, please,' Sloane added.

Sep looked up from the newspaper he was trying to decipher and nodded.

1

'You can't even read that,' Sloane said. 'I don't know why you bother.'

'It's good to try,' her brother replied. He'd been learning Spanish at school and was keen to see if Portuguese was anything like it.

Alice-Miranda noticed the front page. Beneath the headline was a photograph of a grand palace, as well as a collection of candlesticks, paintings and other antiques.

'Excuse me, Mr Perreira. What does that say?' she asked, pointing at the headline.

'Ah, it is a very bad business, Miss Alice-Miranda. The word is *roubado*. It means "stolen",' he said.

'Stolen?' said Alice-Miranda. 'From the palace?'

'Yes, but not just one palace – from *all* the palaces in Sintra,' Mr Perreira explained. 'No one knows how the thieves are getting in and out. The police are looking, but so far they have only come across dead ends.'

'Goodness, I hope nothing's been stolen at the Palace of Pena, where Uncle Lawrence is working,' Alice-Miranda replied.

'Mmm, I think they have lost some very valuable pieces from there,' Mr Perreira said. He leaned in closer and lowered his voice. 'There is talk of tunnels through these mountains.'

Lucas slid into his seat, his plate piled high with bacon, eggs, tomato, baked beans and a side serve of pastries. 'What are you talking about?'

'There's been a bunch of robberies at the palaces in Sintra,' Sep explained.

'Really? Dad's shooting at the Palace of Pena. I can't imagine they'd get in there. Security on movie sets is like trying to break into jail,' Lucas said.

Alice-Miranda shrugged. 'Mr Perreira says they already have.'

'I'm sure the police will catch the thieves soon enough.' Mr Perreira finished pouring the children's juices, then left to greet some arriving guests.

'Speaking of the set, when are we going?' Sloane asked before taking a bite of her buttery toast.

Lucas looked up. 'Dad said today's off limits. They're shooting some mushy love scenes.' He wrinkled his nose. 'But tomorrow there's a battle, so hopefully we can go then. Dad gets to chop off some guy's arm with a sword.'

Sloane pulled a face. 'Oh, that's gross.'

'Yeah, I know. I feel sorry for Charlotte knowing that Dad has to kiss some random woman,' Lucas said. Charlotte Highton-Smith was his stepmother.

'Not that,' Sloane snapped.

'What are you talking about then?' Lucas asked.

'Chopping off someone's arm – *that's* disgusting.' Sloane grimaced.

Lucas grinned. 'It's all just props and makeup, you know. He doesn't really have to chop off an arm.'

'Duh! But it's still gross.'

Alice-Miranda smiled at Sloane. 'I think there's plenty to see around here. Iz, the lovely waitress who served us last night, told me that the ruins of an old monastery and palace are right here in the hotel grounds.'

'Yeah, and there's that church with the domed roof,' Sep added.

Sloane rolled her eyes. 'Boring.'

On the other side of the room, Alice-Miranda's Aunt Charlotte was sitting with Sloane and Sep's parents, September and Smedley Sykes. Charlotte's husband had left early for the Palace of Pena, where his latest movie, an epic drama about the Portuguese royal family, was being filmed. He was playing the lead role of Don Fernando. September Sykes was laughing loudly and fiddling with her mane of platinum hair.

Sep stared at his mother, embarrassment creeping over his face. 'I still can't believe they're here. Does Dad really have business in Lisbon or was that just an excuse for Mum to come and spy on movie stars?'

Sloane shrugged. 'I told Mum you'd be annoyed, but she said that it wasn't fair for you to have all the fun, and besides, it was *only* an eleven-hour drive to get here from Barcelona.'

Lucas and Alice-Miranda swapped smiles. Last night Sep couldn't believe his eyes when his mother had tap-tapped her way towards him across the vast marble foyer of the hotel. When his best friend, Lucas, had asked him to go to Portugal for a week in the school holidays because his father was shooting a movie, Sep had leapt at the chance. It was just a pity that Spain, where Sep's parents lived, was Portugal's geographical neighbour.

Sep's relationship with his mother was tricky at the best of times. He thought that sending him to boarding school was the best decision his parents had ever made. But when his mother hatched an evil plot to bring down his beloved Fayle School, he wondered if he could ever forgive her. At least Sloane seemed to have undergone a radical personal-improvement program in the past few months – probably helped by the fact that she was friends with Alice-Miranda, who was just about the sweetest girl in the world.

September Sykes and Charlotte Highton-Smith walked over to the children's table.

'Are you guys okay to entertain yourselves for a few hours?' Charlotte asked. 'I'm taking September to the day spa.'

September Sykes sighed loudly. 'Look at me. I'm such a mess. I haven't had any pampering in weeks,' she moaned. 'The state of my nails is a disgrace.'

She waved what looked to the others to be perfectly manicured blood-red talons in the air.

'We'll be fine, Aunt Charlotte. We're going exploring,' Alice-Miranda replied.

'That sounds like fun,' Charlotte said. 'Just make sure you stay in the hotel grounds.'

'We will,' the children chorused. That would be easy – there were acres and acres of land, a golf course and all sorts of trails. There was also the monastery and church in the middle of the estate, right opposite the hotel.

Charlotte smiled at the children, then headed off with September. Smedley Sykes remained behind to read the newspaper and enjoy another cup of coffee in peace.

———

The children stood at the front of the hotel.

'Where shall we go first?' Alice-Miranda looked across to the collection of terracotta and mustard-coloured buildings. Rising above the rooftops was the dome of the chapel. It looked as if there was an angel standing on top.

'I'll see if there's a map,' Lucas offered, and scurried back inside to ask the concierge.

Sloane scanned the landscape. 'What's that up there?' She pointed to an oval rock with a large cross on the top, jutting towards the blue sky.

'It's called Penha Longa, the same name as the hotel,' Sep said. 'I read about it. Legend says there's great treasure underneath the rock. The reason the rock has that yellow tinge is because an old woman used to throw eggs at it every day in the hope of cracking it open to get to the treasure. I think she wanted to be a queen or something.'

Sloane frowned. 'That's stupid. As if you could break open a boulder with a few eggs.'

Alice-Miranda stared off into the distance. 'I love stories like that. This place does feel magical, don't you think? Imagine if there really was treasure.'

Lucas reappeared armed with a map. 'Why don't we start in the middle and then follow the trails that lead all the

way around the estate?' he suggested,
pointing out the pathway the concierge
had marked.

Sep, Sloane and Alice-Miranda agreed.

Lucas tucked the map into his pocket,
then sped across towards the set of
steps that led down into a labyrinth of
buildings. The other three raced
after him.

They darted through a courtyard filled
with bronze statues, then rounded the
corner to the front of the chapel. The door
was closed.

'Do you think we can go in?' Sloane
turned the handle, and the door opened.

'It's not locked, so it must be okay,'
Sep said.

Sloane pushed on the heavy door,
which squeaked noisily.

One by one the children entered the cavernous space of whitewashed walls and polished marble arches. A red carpet ran down the aisle with uncomfortable-looking pews on either side. Rays of light beamed through the dome and onto the golden altar below.

'Isn't it lovely?' Alice-Miranda said. She turned and took in the statues of Mary and Jesus positioned on opposite walls. Both were set into the most magnificent carved alcoves.

'It's pretty fancy,' Sloane agreed. 'Nice place for a wedding.'

None of them heard the velvet-slippered footsteps approach. A voice boomed, speaking in Portuguese.

The children spun around to see the source of the outburst – a young priest.

Alice-Miranda stepped forward to greet him. He was wearing black robes and red slippers. A giant gold crucifix hung around his neck. His face was flushed and his eyebrows danced fiercely above dark, piercing eyes.

'I am sorry, Father, but none of us speak Portuguese.' The child smiled. 'My name is Alice-Miranda Highton-Smith-Kennington-Jones and I'm very pleased to meet you,' she said, holding out her hand.

He ignored it, waving the children away. 'You should not be here,' he said in English. 'This is not a playground.'

'We weren't playing,' Sep said. 'We just

14

wanted to have a look at the church, that's all.'

'This place is none of your business,' the priest spat.

'Really?' Sloane eyeballed the man who wasn't much taller than she was. 'I thought everyone was welcome in church.'

'You are not welcome here.' The priest's eyes were wild and specks of spit were gathering in the corner of his mouth.

'But Father, we just wanted to have a look,' Alice-Miranda tried again. 'And the door was unlocked.'

'You need to go. Now!' He ushered them towards the exit.

Sloane stared at the man. 'Keep your hair on,' she blurted, then giggled because the young man really didn't have much hair at all.

The priest grabbed her arm. 'Don't come back here!' he hissed as he dug his long fingernails into her wrist.

'Ow!' Sloane wailed. 'You're hurting me.'

Sep grabbed the priest's arm. 'Let go of my sister.'

'Father, please let go of my friend,' Alice-Miranda said sternly.

'Don't tell me what to do, little girl,' he sneered, but released his grip. 'Now, get out of my church.'

He marched the children to the entrance and pushed the heavy doors shut behind them. The children heard the turning of a key in the lock.

'You're in trouble, you know,' Sloane called out. 'As soon as my mother hears about what you did you'll be sorry!' She rubbed her forearm.

'Did you see his nails? He had a better manicure than our mother,' Sep said.

'I've never met a priest like him before,' Lucas said, frowning. 'I wonder what he's hiding.'

Alice-Miranda wondered as well. She had a strange feeling about the man.

'Wait until I tell Mum. She'll go ballistic, and I'm sure the manager of the hotel will have something to say to him too,' Sloane huffed. 'You can't push children around like that.'

Lucas retrieved the map from his pocket. 'Forget about him. Let's go and find some of those ruins.'

The children scampered off between the buildings and headed down another set of

stairs. To their right was the golf course
and to their left there was an old roadway.
The sun filtered through branches of
an overhanging tree, creating speckled
patterns on the ground. Not far along, the
children were rewarded with their first
ancient building. It looked like some sort
of fort, and inside its walls was a large
rectangular pool. You couldn't see the
bottom through the murky water.

'This is lovely,' Alice-Miranda breathed.

Sloane screwed up her nose. 'I wouldn't
want to swim in there.'

'I don't think it's a swimming pool,'
Sep said. 'It's probably just for decoration.
I bet this place was for ceremonies or
something.'

The children split up and explored
every nook and cranny until Sloane

decided she'd had enough and wanted
to see what else they could find.

Further along the road a squat building
with a terracotta roof and an empty moat
came into view. Walls, in various states
of decay, rose above the children. The
building didn't look nearly as old as the
first one and, with its shuttered windows,
seemed to be locked up tight.

Sloane tried the doorhandle. This time
she was disappointed.

'I don't think that's a good idea,
anyway,' Sep said. 'You know what
happened last time we went inside.'

'You'd have to be unlucky to run into
that grumpy priest again,' Lucas said with
a smile. 'I'd love to know what's in there.'

Sloane walked around the side of the
building and was surprised to find steps

leading down into the ground. 'Hey, I think I've found a cellar,' she called to the others. 'It's probably a secret tunnel or something.'

Alice-Miranda, Sep and Lucas ran around to join her.

Sep studied the doorway. There was a door but no lock. He ran his hands over the peeling paint.

Sloane looked at her brother. 'I was *joking*. As if you're going to find anything.'

There was a loud click, followed by a grating sound. They all stared in amazement as the door swung open. An eerie glow was coming from inside.

Sep grinned and winked. 'Just call me Bond, James Bond.'

The children looked at each other.

'Come on,' Lucas said. 'We'll just take a peek.'

'Maybe we shouldn't,' Sloane whispered.

'It's probably a storeroom for the hotel or something,' Sep said, taking a step forward.

One by one the children made their way down the steps, which narrowed the further they went. Sloane was secretly relieved that at least it was getting brighter.

'Whoa, this place is mad,' Lucas said when they finally reached the bottom. He squinted into the passageway lined with blazing candles. 'It looks like something out of a movie.'

'Don't you think it's a bit weird that there are candles burning under the ground?' Sloane said, feeling uneasy.

'Iz said that the hotel sometimes uses the ruins for events. It could be set up for a lunch or something,' Alice-Miranda offered.

'Creepy place to have lunch, if you ask me.' Sloane shuddered.

The children walked in single file with Sep leading the way. They continued on for about thirty metres when the boy suddenly put up his hand to indicate for them to stop. 'Adventure's over,' he announced.

Up ahead, the passage came to an abrupt stop.

'That's strange,' Alice-Miranda said. She stood next to Sep. 'Do you think there could be another secret door?'

They both ran their hands over the surface of the wall, but nothing happened.

'I'll give you a leg-up,' Lucas suggested. 'Maybe it's higher this time.' He leaned down and cupped his hands together.

'Okay,' Alice-Miranda said. 'I'm not very heavy.'

Lucas hoisted her up while Sep steadied her from behind. And as she ran her tiny hands over the top of the masonry, she found a loose brick.

'This might be something,' Alice-Miranda said as she pressed down on the brick. There was a horrible grating sound, then a few moments later the wall turned sideways. 'Wow!' she gasped.

The children crept through the pivoted wall. The passage continued for another fifty metres or so before it opened into a large chamber. If the secret wall was unexpected, what they found next was a complete surprise.

There were silver candelabras, oil paintings and beautiful porcelain vases and urns lined up against the walls.

'What's all this?' Lucas's eyes were on stalks as he took in the vast array of treasures.

Alice-Miranda walked among the items, inspecting them more closely.

'This vase looks like one I've seen in Granny's house. I'm not allowed anywhere near it.'

All of a sudden the candles on the walls flickered.

Sloane spun around searching for the source of the draught. 'What was that?'

There were mumbling voices coming from the other side of the chamber and they seemed to be getting closer. The children froze.

'What is the problem now?' one of the voices demanded. 'You can have a look at the goods, but they must be gone by tonight. You know the deal.'

Alice-Miranda motioned to the others, and the four children scurried into the far corner, where they ducked behind one of the paintings. She wondered where she'd heard that voice before. The man's English was heavily accented – it was definitely not his native language.

'Twenty million euros,' another voice said. He sounded American.

'That was our agreement,' the first man replied.

The children held their breath as the men walked among the goods.

'You have done well, Father,' said the American. 'My employer will be pleased. And your disguise – it has worked wonders.'

Sloane gulped. 'The priest,' she mouthed.

The children looked at each other and nodded.

'Have you seen enough?' the priest demanded.

There was a grunt and the sound of footsteps moving away. Only one pair made no sound.

'Tonight, you will use the other entrance. I hope your truck is well camouflaged.'

'We have a van with the hotel logo. No one will suspect workmen doing repairs.'

'Excellent.'

The children stayed put several minutes longer before they emerged from their hiding place.

'There must be another entrance,' Alice-Miranda said. 'It was lucky they didn't come the same way we did, or they'd have found us for sure.'

Sep walked among the treasures. 'This must be all the stuff from the palaces.'

'What are *you* doing here?' a voice boomed. 'How dare you!'

The children jumped like startled rabbits. It was the priest. He mustn't have left with the other man.

'We know what you're up to,' Sep blurted. 'You'll never get away with it.'

The young man glared at Sep. 'How are you planning to stop me exactly?' He reached into his robe and pulled out a nail file.

'What's that for? Are you going to give us manicures?' Sloane hissed.

'You may mock me, but I will enjoy making you suffer,' the priest threatened. 'And this thing is much sharper than it looks.'

Sloane gulped.

Alice-Miranda looked around. There had to be a way to distract him. They needed to get out of there and call the police.

'Move it!' the priest demanded. 'I have the perfect place to lock you away, where all they will find is your bones.'

Alice-Miranda nudged Lucas. She stared at the vase and gave a nod.

'You might want to catch this first!' Lucas picked up the vase and threw it at the priest.

'What are you doing, you idiot!' he bellowed, diving to catch it. He hit the ground just as the vase thudded into his outstretched arms.

The nail file flew across the passage. Sep raced to pick it up.

'Noooooo!' the priest cried out.

Lucas leapt onto the man's back, pinning him to the ground.

Sep scrambled back to the group and put the file into his pocket. 'Quick, find something to tie him up,' he said. 'What about the boxes over there? Is there some tape?'

Sloane and Alice-Miranda hurried over
to have a look.

'Found some!' Alice-Miranda called
out. She quickly found the end of the
roll while Lucas grabbed the man's
wrists behind his back. 'Stay still,
please,' Alice-Miranda said. 'We're
going to tie you up whether you like
it or not.'

The man continued to struggle but
Lucas, Alice-Miranda and Sloane managed
to wind the tape around his arms. Then
they taped his ankles too.

'You can't do this to me. There
are people who will come after you!'
he spat.

Lucas rolled him onto his back while
Sloane took the tape from Lucas and bit
off a small piece, which she slapped over

the man's mouth. 'I told you not to push kids around,' she said, glaring into his wild eyes. 'You think *I'm* bad? Just wait until my mother gets hold of you.'

'You and Sep get help, Alice-Miranda,' Lucas said. 'We'll watch the *priest.*'

It wasn't long before Alice-Miranda and Sep returned with Mr Perreira and the hotel manager in tow.

'Goodness!' the hotel manager exclaimed as he walked among the stolen goods. 'This is unbelievable.'

'We thought so too,' said Alice-Miranda.

'But how did you catch him?' Mr Perreira looked at the children.

'It was Alice-Miranda.' Lucas smiled at his young cousin. 'You can thank her, although you might not have if the priest's reflexes hadn't been so good.'

Mr Perreira frowned. He looked at Alice-Miranda, whose brown eyes sparkled.

'We'll tell you all about it later,' Lucas said as the wailing of police sirens could be heard in the distance.

FREAK
BY TRISTAN BANCKS

'Roll up! Roll up! He's the most hideous freak you have ever laid eyes on! He's disgusting! He's disgraceful! He will make you vomit!'

'Settle down,' I whisper to Jack through the thin red curtain.

'What?' Jack asks, poking his head inside. 'You don't have to say they'll vomit.'

Jack rolls his eyes and shuts the curtain. 'You will not vomit!' he announces in the same ringmaster voice. He goes on to use words like 'gasp' and 'horror' and, 'This lunchtime only. Just two dollars!'

I am sitting inside a small red teepee that Jack and I have built under the trees at the far end of the bottom playground. The teepee is made of long, straight branches and a red sheet from my house.

Jack thinks this pop-up freak show will make us wealthy beyond our wildest dreams, and I need cash to buy a birthday present for Sasha, something that will convince her to go out with me again. I want to prove to her that I'm not selfish and weird like she says.

'You ready for the first customer?' Jack asks, poking his head back inside.

I look at my socked foot, nervous.

'I guess,' I say.

Jack whips open the curtain and says, 'Welcome! Welcome!'

Brent Bunder appears. He is a giant
bulldozer of a kid with diggers for hands.
He fills the teepee.

'Take a seat,' I squeak.

Brent Bunder lowers himself
awkwardly onto one of the kindergarten
chairs we have borrowed. It strains and
moans under his weight.

'This better be good,' he grunts. He is
red-faced and sweaty, like he just guzzled
a bottle of hot chilli sauce. He looks
uncomfortable, crammed into the tiny
space. I want to run but I can hear Jack
outside dropping another coin into his
lunch box.

So I slowly peel my limp, grey sock
down over my ankle. Over my heel. Down
my foot. Brent watches on as I close my
eyes and reveal my toes.

Silence.

I open one eye.

And there it is.

My foot.

One. Two. Three. Four.

Four toes. Slightly webbed. Like a cartoon duck. It has been that way since birth. I have never really shown anyone apart from Jack and my family. My sister says it is proof that I'm a mutant from another planet.

Brent Bunder looks on, expressionless.

'There are only four,' I explain helpfully. Brent Bunder isn't exactly top of our year in maths.

Still nothing.

'There are meant to be five,' I say.

He pokes my toes with one gigantic finger, like he is checking that they are real, that I haven't bought them from a magic shop.

Eventually he says, 'So what? You're deformed. Is that what I paid two bucks for? Now I can't buy an iceblock, and I'm hot.'

'Well . . .' I say, looking up at him. He does look hot. His face is speckled with tiny beads of sweat.

'I want my money back.'

'Sure. No problem,' I say.

Jack's face appears through the gap in the sheet behind Brent. He shakes his head and mouths the words, 'No way.'

I look at Brent. Angry, sweaty, bulldozer Brent. He could crush me like a can. How can I make this worth two dollars?

'Would you believe a bear bit it off?' I say, half-joking.

'What?'

'Well . . .' My mind whirrs, scanning for ideas. 'When I was little we lived in Canada and . . . I was two years old and playing down by the creek at the back of my house, and this . . . black bear, a big one, came along and . . .'

Brent Bunder looks totally suspicious.

'And he started growling at me, but he was over the other side of the creek. And I crawled away but this grizzly —'

'You said it was a black bear,' Brent says.

'This black bear started swimming across the creek, and when he reached my side he . . . attacked me,' I explain.

'Attacked?'

'Well, he bit me. On the foot. Bit the toe clean off. My mum heard screaming and she ran down to the creek. When she saw the blood dripping down the bear's chin and the missing toe, she fainted and –'

'Bears have chins?' Brent questions.

'Well, yeah, the furry bit just below their mouth.' Brent leans forward, looking me in the eye. 'And my big sister picked me up and ran two k's to the hospital, and they stitched me up. That's why the toes are sort of webbed. Because of the stitches.'

Brent fixes me with a distant look, like he's replaying parts of the story in his mind. 'What happened to the bear?' he asks.

'Um . . . I don't know. It went off into the forest and . . . maybe it ate some other kid's toe. Maybe it wanted the complete set,' I suggest. 'Y'know. Collect all five!'

I hold his glare, waiting for him to punch me really hard in the nose or rip the teepee apart in a rage. But, instead, he says, 'You're a freak, mate. I love it.' He stands and turns to go. 'Oh, by the way, I want a third of the profits.'

'Why?'

'Because I'm big and you're small.'

'Fair enough,' I say.

'I'll be back at the end of lunch to collect.' Then he ducks outside. 'It's awesome!' he announces to the other kids. 'You wait till you hear how it happened.'

And that is it. From then on, I am unstoppable. I tell each kid a different story and swear them to secrecy. The tales get taller every time.

'A shark bit it off,' I tell Morgan Brett.

'As if. How?' he asks.

'My dad's a fisherman. For the first two years of my life we lived on a trawler at sea, and one day he netted a shark about a metre-and-a-half, two metres long.'

'Get out.'

'The shark slipped out of the net and slid across the boat's deck. I was crawling around, playing with my jack-in-the-box, and the shark's mouth came to rest right near my foot.'

His eyes widen. I make a chomping sound and a snapping motion with my hands. Morgan is gobsmacked.

'Next!' Jack shouts.

And so it goes.

I tell Millie Randall my toe was trapped in a piece of machinery.

Another kid, that a flesh-eating disease rotted it off.

Caught in the spokes of a motorbike.

Trampled by a horse's hoof.

Hacked off by a chainsaw.

Lost in a bet.

Jack warns me to pull back on the stories, but I'm on a roll. By the time the last kid leaves the teepee near the end of lunch, we have fifty-eight dollars in cold, hard change. For the first time in his life, Jack was right: we are rich!

I have just started packing up the chairs when Sasha pokes her head into the teepee.

Sasha. The cutest girl in Australia. My ex-girlfriend.

'Hey, Tom,' she says, real sweet. White jumper, hair in a ponytail, eyes like blue sky.

'Hi,' I say.

'What's the freaky thing that everyone's talking about?'

'Nothin'.'

'I want to know. I've paid my money.'

There is no way I can show Sasha my freaky foot.

'Jack, we have to make a refund,' I call out. 'The bell's about to go.'

Jack pokes his head through the curtain next to Sasha. 'It's okay. We still have time.'

'No we don't.'

'Yes we do.'

'Don't.'

'Do.' He mouths the word 'sixty' to me.

Sixty bucks. That's how much we will have if I show Sasha my missing toe. A nice round sixty. Twenty for Jack, twenty for me, twenty for Brent Bunder, the filthy scoundrel. Four weeks' pocket money for one hour's work. Enough to buy Sasha's present.

'Are you going to show me or not?' she asks.

'Just give me a moment,' I say.

I slip out of the teepee to find Jack and Brent waiting for me.

'I am not showing Sasha,' I say.

'Show her or I'm keeping the money,' Jack replies.

'What?'

'It was my idea.'

'It's my foot!'

Brent makes a throat-slitting motion with one of his giant sausage fingers and points towards the teepee.

So I scowl and go inside.

I sit down.

Me and Sasha. And the toe. The missing toe.

'What's so bad?' she asks.

'You'll see.'

I start to peel the sock down.

What should I tell her? The truth? Or one of my stories? I don't want to mess this up. I don't want to ruin my plan of marrying Sasha and having three kids and a Labradoodle and a house overlooking the ocean with secret passages and revolving bookcases.

Over the ankle, over the heel.

Don't do it, I think.

Sasha looks on, fascinated.

Over the foot, over the toes and . . .

There they are in all their freakish glory.

Boom.

Sasha stares. Little creases appear in her forehead.

'How did it happen?' she asks quietly.

Um, I think. I don't want to lie to her but she deserves a good story, a better story than anyone, just for being Sasha. 'I was born like that' just isn't worth two dollars. So I open up my mind and the story seems to fall from the sky.

'When I was four my sister's guinea pig escaped from its hutch,' I say, intense, serious. 'But this was no ordinary guinea

pig. It was *twice* the size of a regular one.
Feral. I think she found it in the bush.
I was in the sandpit playing cars one day
and I heard its claws on the concrete
path. I turned and saw it coming for me.
I backed off into the corner of the pit.
I threw a Matchbox car at the beast, but
it just raised a paw and batted it away.
I screamed but Mum was out front
cleaning the car and didn't hear me.
It climbed up on the wooden edge of the
sandpit and reared up on its back legs,
like a wrestler ready to launch himself off
the top turnbuckle. I freaked and
ran. It chased me across the
grass, up the back steps and
halfway across the verandah,
then it pounced, ripping
my toe out of the socket

with its razor-sharp teeth. I screamed
and clutched my foot as it retreated to its
hutch to pick the flesh off the bone and
digest its gruesome meal.'

Sasha stares, open-mouthed.

I breathe hard. I have given it everything.
It is a story worth five bucks, not two. It is
a movie, really. Dreamworks will probably
want to buy the rights. It is the greatest
story about a feral guinea pig ever told.

I look at her.

She smiles. She looks so beautiful it
hurts.

'That's a lie,' she says.

'Huh?'

'Tell me what really happened. Were
you just born like that?'

I feel like an idiot. So I say the obvious
thing: 'No. That's what really happened.'

'Tom,' she says, trying to make me smile. But I won't. I'm in too deep now. I have to see this through. Otherwise she will think I am a liar, and she will never marry me, and we will never own a Labradoodle.

'That's the truth,' I say.

She shakes her head. 'Why would you look me in the eye and lie to me, tell me such a dumb story.'

Dumb! She actually says the word 'dumb'.

'And then you don't even have the guts to admit you made it up.'

'But I didn't!'

Sasha stands. 'Jack was right. You are hideous. Not your toes. Just you.'

'But –'

She vanishes through the curtain. I chase her.

'How'd that go?' Jack asks.

'Yeah. Great,' I say, pushing past him.

'Sasha!' I call, but she's walking off across the playground and out of my life.

'I'm telling everyone you're a liar!' she shouts. 'You'll have to pay every cent back.'

'Wait. Sasha. Please!'

She keeps walking. I've blown it. This is the worst moment of my life, until . . .

I feel a heavy hand on my shoulder. It spins me around.

'I want my money. Now.' It's Brent Bunder. He is not smiling.

'But —'

Jack is standing just behind Brent. Jack pulls the elastic waistband on his track pants forward and pours all the money out of his lunch box and into his undies.

'You . . . idiot!' I say. I can't help it.

Brent turns to Jack, and Jack starts running away with all the money. I twist out of Brent's grip and sprint across the playground – one shoe on, one shoe off. Brent gives chase. I hit the basketball courts, my bare, webbed foot slapping against the tar. I catch up with Jack and we bolt towards the front gate of the school. Jack's underpants are jingling like mad.

'You're scrubbing that money clean,' I snarl at him and look back to see Jonah Flem, Morgan Brett, Millie Randall and Brent Bunder racing after us. And, further back, Sasha, standing with her arms crossed. My classmates, the girl I love and the school's resident giant are after my blood.

'You're dead!' Brent Bunder screams.

So Jack and I keep running – a cheap sideshow freak and a scam artist. As we pick up speed, the coins begin to rain down from Jack's pant legs, leaving a golden trail of lies and broken dreams.

We stop at the gate to catch our breath. Jonah, Morgan, Millie and Brent are grabbing all the coins off the ground and stuffing them into their pockets.

'We're rich!' Morgan shouts.

'Bonehead!' Jack says, and he kicks me. As he does, one last coin drops from the leg of his pants to the ground, and I swoop on it before he does.

'Gimme that!' Jack demands, but I back away quickly, rubbing the moisture off the coin and holding it up in the sunshine. Our last two bucks. It glints like

a magical nugget of hope . . . and it fills
me with a possibly brilliant idea.

'Do you reckon, if I bought Sasha a
sausage roll with sauce for her birthday,
that'd be enough to make her want to go
out with me again?'

Jack growls, runs at me and mashes me
into the ground.

ZAFARIN'S CHALLENGE

BY ALEESAH DARLISON

From the shadows, hands seized Zafarin and dragged him into the alleyway. An arm wound around his waist while a hand locked over his mouth.

'Calm down, Zaf!' a voice hissed. 'It's me.'

Zafarin relaxed and was released. 'What are you doing, Dane?'

'Aren't you happy to see your brother?'

'Not when he frightens me to death,' Zafarin huffed.

'Shush!' Dane glanced behind him. 'Follow me and I'll tell you what this is all about.'

Intrigued, Zafarin followed his brother through the city's murky cobblestone laneways. Dane stopped outside a tumbledown house. He glanced around and then led Zafarin inside.

Dane showed Zafarin through a concealed doorway beneath the staircase, then down into a dimly lit cellar. Zafarin studied his brother in the candlelight. He hadn't seen him for four years. His knight's uniform, royal blue with a gold eagle emblazoned across the front, was clean and freshly pressed. His thick hair was long and shiny. A battle scar ran across Dane's left cheek from his nose to his ear, adding an air of mystery to his features.

'He don't half look like you,' a voice sounded nearby.

'I told you, Dogan,' Dane said.

Zafarin noticed two other knights seated at a table in the corner. One had red hair and a red beard and was demolishing a bowl of stew. The other had black hair and a thin moustache. He was as slender as his companion was round.

'Ain't as big as you, though,' Dogan replied. 'Can he fight?'

Zafarin glared. 'Anyone care to tell me what's going on?'

'It's good to see you, brother.' Dane grinned as he hugged Zafarin. 'Are Mum and Dad well?'

'They're fine,' Zafarin said. 'What's this all about?'

'Good old Zaf,' Dane said. 'Always to the point. So, here it is. Wrindarn, the evil wizard, has invaded the city and locked King Ronan in the dungeon. He's cast a spell on everyone in the palace. Our fellow knights included.

'It was pure luck that Dogan, Brax and I were on a scouting mission and so escaped Wrindarn's spell. We haven't been noticed missing yet, but soon will be. There's a feast at the palace tonight in honour of the Grim Valley Battle. We're expected to attend.'

'You can't return to the palace,' Zafarin said. 'It's too dangerous.'

'We know that,' Dane said. 'Which is why you're going in my place while I search for Mogdan, the Grand Warlock, who will defeat Wrindarn.'

'Me in your place?' Zafarin's heart thudded. 'I can't. You're a knight, a hero. I'm an actor's apprentice, a performer.'

'Precisely,' Dane said. 'You look like me *and* you're an actor.'

'*Apprentice* actor,' Zafarin corrected him. He shook his head, trying to understand. 'So you want me to dress up as a knight and enjoy a feast?'

Dane winced. 'Not exactly. While you're there you must steal Wrindarn's key and use it to free the king. He must escape the palace before midnight when Wrindarn's spell will take full effect. Otherwise, King Ronan will fall asleep for a thousand years. Wrindarn will seize power and our kingdom will be lost.'

'You'd be better at rescuing the King,' Zafarin said. 'I could search for

Mogdan instead. That would be safer for everyone.'

'Dane has another mission,' Brax explained. 'Wrindarn intends marrying the King's daughter, Princess Freena, at midnight. Dane has to smuggle the princess out of the city and take her to safety in the Emerald Mountains.'

Zafarin laughed. 'You always did like practical jokes, Dane, but this one beats them all.'

'I'm not joking,' Dane said. 'We need your help, Zaf. The kingdom of Ilsan depends on you.'

'I don't believe you.' Zafarin crossed his arms.

'Will you believe me?' A girl slid out from the shadows. Although she wore a peasant's dress, her coal-black

hair and regal features were instantly
recognisable.

'Your Highness.' Zafarin bowed.
'I don't know what to say.'

'Say you'll help us.' She placed a
delicate hand in Dane's.

Instantly, Zafarin knew how things
were between Dane and the princess.
He also knew he couldn't deny her, so he
hastily swapped clothes with Dane. 'How
do I look?'

'The resemblance is uncanny,' Brax said.

'There's only one thing missing,' Princess Freena said. 'The scar.'

'Some actor's paint will fix that.' Zafarin searched his cloak, which Dane now wore. He pulled out a small tub. 'This should do the trick.'

Zafarin fashioned himself a fake scar to resemble Dane's. As everyone was agreeing that Zafarin made a fine knight, a bell chimed nine o'clock.

'We have to go,' Dane said. 'So do you, Zaf.'

Dane and Princess Freena departed on horseback while Dogan, Brax and Zafarin walked to the palace. His back rigid with fear and his legs threatening to collapse beneath him, Zafarin entered the grand hall alongside Dogan and Brax. All the elements of a celebration were present, only no one seemed to be enjoying themselves.

Zafarin and the others sat at a table, pretending to be at ease. All the while, they kept a lookout for Wrindarn. Time trickled away.

Finally, a tall, dark-haired man with piercing saffron eyes strode into the room. 'Welcome, brave warriors!' he cried. 'Tonight you witness the dawn of a new era. The evil tyrant Ronan has been overthrown. From now on, you owe your loyalty to me, King Wrindarn!'

The knights clapped mechanically. No one challenged Wrindarn. Dogan growled under his breath.

Zafarin glanced at the clock.

Eleven-thirty. He took a deep breath and stood up. A glazed look, like the one worn by the other knights, overcame Zafarin's features.

'Hail, King Wrindarn,' Zafarin said. 'I am D-Dane Fierceforce and I offer myself to you as your protector.'

'Ah, Fierceforce, I've heard about you. Bow to your new master.'

As Zafarin bowed obediently, he noticed a key hanging from Wrindarn's wrist. 'May I kiss your hand, master?'

Wrindarn nodded. Zafarin took Wrindarn's hand and bent to kiss it, deftly sliding the key chain from the wizard's

arm as he did so. With the key concealed in his sleeve, Zafarin turned and melted into the throng. Dogan and Brax followed.

'I've got the key,' Zafarin said.

'To the dungeon,' Brax said. 'Before Wrindarn realises it's missing.'

'It's almost midnight.' Dogan nodded towards the clock.

Down the hallways they raced until they came to a dragon slumbering in front of the dungeon door.

Zafarin's stomach clenched. 'Dane didn't say anything about a dragon.'

'He didn't know about it.' Dogan's face was stiff with terror. 'None of us did.'

'I'm terrified of dragons,' Brax squeaked.

'Don't knights fight dragons all the time?' Zafarin said.

Brax shook his head. 'Usually we just get eaten by them.'

'I'll go,' Zafarin sighed, and tiptoed past the sleeping dragon. When he reached the door, he slipped the key into the lock and turned it. The dragon didn't stir. Zafarin found the king inside. As he led him into the hallway the door swung on its hinges, creaking loudly.

The dragon woke. Its red eyes glowed like rubies. It shot towards Zafarin and the king, pinning them against the wall. The beast drew its head back and snorted fire. Zafarin jumped out of the way seconds before he was turned into charcoal.

'Brax, Dogan, distract the dragon!' Zafarin shouted as he dodged the hot blasts.

The knights waved their swords. The dragon lunged, sending them scattering. 'Aaaagggghhhh!'

At the same time, Zafarin ran behind the dragon, waving his arms and shouting. Frustrated and not knowing which way to turn, the clumsy monster blasted fire all around at its tormentors. Through the flames and the smoke, Zafarin saw his chance. The dragon's tail had flicked inside the dungeon doorway. Zafarin slammed the heavy door shut. The dragon let out an agonised roar.

It was stuck fast.

'Quick, before it breaks free!' Zafarin urged the others down the corridor.

They ran towards the stables and saddled their horses. The clock chimed midnight as they galloped out of the palace gates.

Just in time! Zafarin thought.

Several hours later, the king was reunited with his daughter.

'Thank goodness you're safe.' Princess Freena hugged her father.

'And you, my daughter. You were right about Dane being a man of honour. It appears his brother is also.'

Zafarin blushed. 'It was nothing.'

'We must swap places again,' Dane told Zafarin. 'Now the king's safe, Dogan, Brax and I will return to the palace with Mogdan to fight Wrindarn. You stay here with the others. We'll send for you when all is safe.'

'Won't you need my help?' Zafarin asked.

'Aren't you afraid?' Mogdan asked.

'I was at first,' Zafarin said, 'but I guess I got over it. Actually, I've never felt so . . . alive.'

'Nor so close to death,' murmured Dogan.

Zafarin laughed. 'Well, that, too.'

'Zafarin has proven his bravery,' King Ronan said. 'He'd be a valuable support, I'm sure.'

'All right.' Dane nodded. 'We leave immediately.'

With a beat of hooves and a cloud of dust, the knights, Zafarin and Mogdan set off for the city. Despite the danger facing them, Zafarin couldn't help feeling excited.

THE HAUNTED BUDGIE

BY COLIN THOMPSON

George the budgerigar was depressed.
Everyone in the whole world was having a
better time than he was. The old rat under
the sink was having more fun than he was.
Even the fleas in the rat's ears had more
fun than him. Even the blind slugs in the
deepest cellars who had nothing to eat
but really old slime and who kept getting
trodden on by blind giants, had a more
fulfilling life than he did. His cage was in
the dampest darkest corner of the kitchen

and it had been put there deliberately. No one talked to him anymore except to tell him to shut up when he told them all what a pretty boy he was.

'If I just dropped dead right now,' he said, 'no one would care. They'd just stick me in an old carrier bag with the dog's hair and chuck me in the dustbin.'

'Don't be so pathetic,' said the ghost in his mirror.

'Or they'd chuck me on the compost heap,' he moaned, 'and bury me under the potato peelings.'

'I can't stand any more of this,' said the ghost. 'I'm off to haunt the shaving mirror in the bathroom.'

'That's it,' said George, 'go off and leave me. Everyone else has.'

———

George the budgerigar was depressed
and the more he sat and sulked, the
angrier he got. He swore under his breath,
crashed up and down on his perch and
kicked lumps out of his cuttlefish.
He was furious and there is nothing more
dangerous in the whole world than an
angry budgerigar. At least that's what
George told himself.

'They'll be sorry,' he muttered.
'They'll wish they'd been nicer to me,
by the time I'm finished with them.'

'Oh, yeah,' said the spider that lived in
the top of his cage. 'What are you going to
do, spill your millet on the floor?'

'I'll show them,' said George.

He knew there wasn't really anything
he could do but he was so furious he
wasn't thinking clearly. It was midnight

and everyone had gone off to bed leaving the light on.

'They probably did it deliberately,' said George, 'just to keep me awake all night.'

He glared at the light with all the anger his little body could muster. The dirty yellow globe was a symbol of everything horrible that had ever been done to him. It was a mean pale copy of the sun but it gave him no warmth. He narrowed his eyes and stared right into the light bulb and then something wonderful happened.

The light bulb exploded.

Wow, telekinesis, he thought. But as he fell asleep in the peaceful darkness he thought it was probably just a coincidence.

As the sun crept in through the curtains the next morning, George looked at its light glinting in all the pieces of broken glass on the kitchen table and he knew it hadn't just been an accident. He knew he'd made it happen.

He shattered a wine glass on the draining board just to make sure, and then made the whole roll of paper towels unravel onto the floor.

'This is more like it,' he said.

A few ghosts were fiddling about in the corner and George made a wooden spoon fly right through them. They flew behind the bread bin and peered out into the apparently empty room.

'No more mister nice guy,' said George. 'From now on I'm the king of the kitchen.' And he opened and closed his cage door a few times to prove it.

He could have escaped, flown right away to freedom. The window was

wide open enough. But, no, it was
going to be more fun staying where
he was.

Before he took on the world, he had to
develop his powers. He tried to open the
oven but it was too heavy, and he managed
to turn on the cold tap but the hot one
was turned off too tightly. It would
take practice and self-discipline until he
realised his full potential. And, as proud as
he was of his new powers, he would have
to make sure he didn't tell anyone, not
even his best friend.

But he didn't have a best friend, he
realised, getting angry again. He didn't
even have a worst friend. So he decided to
break the rest of the wine glasses and pull
all the petals off all the flowers in the vase
to cheer himself up.

When the family came down for breakfast and found all the mess, they just assumed it was the ghosts. As they cleaned up the mess, George taunted them by telling them what a pretty boy he was but they just told him to shut up.

'Shut up, is it?' he said to himself. 'I'll give them shut up.' And he turned off the fridge.

By lunchtime someone noticed water leaking out of the fridge door and the family spent all afternoon shouting at each other.

'It'll end in tears,' said Granny, and for once she was right.

Peter and Alice, neither of whom could actually reach the switch, were both blamed for it. After all, who else could have done it?

'It must have been the ghosts,' said Peter, but all the ghosts denied it.

'You always believe the ghosts,' said Alice to their parents. 'It must have been one of them.'

George felt a bit sorry for the children but it only lasted a hundredth of a second. It was them who had put him in the dark corner and it was them who always forgot to clean out the bottom of his cage. And thinking of the bottom of his cage gave him an idea: all those horrible wet seed husks and tiny black-and-white droppings.

Well, well! he thought. *It looks like muesli, just like it.*

———

That night it took George over an hour to get the lid off the muesli container and another two hours to make everything fly out of the bottom of his cage and drop

into the jar. After that it
took an hour to
mix it all up
and spread a
thin layer of oats
and raisins on the top, and finally another
hour to get the lid back on. It was almost
dawn by the time he had finished and he
was exhausted, but it had been worth
it. He broke the new light bulb, fell
asleep and dreamed that he was back
in the outback flying through the trees
with thousands of his relations.

Of course, the ghosts got the blame for
the muesli and the second light bulb, and
when they told the humans it had been
George, no one believed them.

'Come on,' said Mum. 'Look at him,
he's just a stupid budgie.'

George jumped up and down and pecked his mirror and looked as dim as he could. 'Who's a pretty boy? Who's a pretty boy?' he said, and pretended to fall off his perch.

'See,' said Dad. 'He can't even sit on his perch without tripping over his feet.'

Morons, thought George.

———

After a week of breaking light bulbs and chucking food around, George decided it was time for bigger and better things. He was fed up with spilling people's tea and reckoned it was time to leave his familiar cage. It was time to come out and play.

As soon as everyone was asleep he opened his cage door and flew into the hall. It was a full moon and everywhere was lit up with a cool blue light. Outside, the town was silent apart from the distant sound of a few early morning cars.

Outside, thought George. *Maybe I should fly away!* But it wasn't time to chase freedom; it was time for revenge.

———

Upstairs he could hear Granny snoring. She sounded like an old lion with a bad cold. George flew into the lounge room and turned on the television and the radio and the hi-fi, and the radio in the kitchen and the television in Peter's room and the television in Alice's room and the alarm clock beside their parents' bed. Dad was in the shower before he realised it was still dark outside. Mum was on her way downstairs to let the dog out before

she realised it was only two o'clock in
the morning.

'This is great,' said George, shutting off
the hot tap and catching Peter's dad with a
sudden blast of icy cold water.

———

Every night George thought up more
nasty tricks to play on the family who
had treated him so badly.

'I'll teach them not to love me,'
he said. 'I'm a pretty boy. Who's a pretty
boy? Me!'

And every morning it was the ghosts
who got the blame. By now the ghosts
knew it was George causing all the havoc,
but of course no one would believe them.

'He's just a stupid budgie,' insisted
Mum.

George jumped up and down and pecked his mirror. 'Who's a pretty boy? Who's a pretty boy?' he said and was laughing so much he really did fall off his perch.

'See,' said Dad. 'He can't even sit on his perch without tripping over his feet.'

This is brilliant, thought George.

'Look, we know it's one of you ghosts,' said Mum, 'and if you don't stop it, we'll get the exorcise bike out and get rid of the lot of you.'

That night the ghosts had a meeting.

'We've got to do something about this wretched bird or we'll all be homeless,' said Elvira, Queen of the Witches.

'The trouble is,' said the Toothbrush Fairy, 'he's not frightened of any of us.'

'What we have to do,' said Bert, the Ghoul of the Breadbin, 'is make the humans catch him at it.'

The curtains flew open. Something fluttered across the window and a squeaky voice asked them who was a pretty boy.

'Damn,' said Elvira, 'that miserable bird's been listening to every word we've said.'

George made a CD fly across the room and slot into the hi-fi. It was a Welsh male voice choir, and as it blared out through the house, the ghosts fled in terror.

The budgie flew after them, taunting loudly, 'Who's a pretty clever boy? Who's a pretty clever boy?'

The music had woken up Nigel the old dog, and he was blundering around the kitchen, banging into the furniture.

Stupid animal, thought George, and tipped a jar of honey over him. Nigel spent the rest of the night licking his coat until all the honey was inside him, apart from the nice, even layer on Peter's bed and clothes and carpet and wallpaper.

———

For two weeks George flew round the house every night creating chaos. The ghosts persuaded Mum to lock the kitchen door and take away the key but George just concentrated hard until the lock opened. Just for good measure, he took the door off and made the hinges fly down the garden into the harbour.

After a fortnight, George began to get bored. There were only so many light bulbs you could explode, only so many times you could wake everyone up before it stopped being fun.

Maybe it's time to go outside, he thought.

He lifted the letterbox and looked out into the night. It was cold outside, too cold for a small bird that should have been living in tropical Australia, but a voice inside him told him to fly away. So he did.

'Got him,' said Elvira, Queen of the Witches as she tied up the letterbox with more string than even the most telepathic budgie could undo. 'By the time he gets half that lot undone, he'll have frozen to death,' she said. 'Serves him right,' said the Toothbrush Fairy. 'Yes, but then he'll be a ghost,' said Ensor the Demon of the Drains, 'and he'll come and live with us.'

'Damn,' said Elvira, 'I hadn't thought of that.' They spent the next twenty minutes undoing all the string and swearing at each other.

'What are we going to do?' said the Toothbrush Fairy.

'We'll talk to Alice,' said Elvira. 'She'll believe us and she'll think of something.'

'She won't believe us, no one does,' said Ensor.

But she did and she was a wise child and had been wondering why George, who had been such a chirpy bird, had suddenly become so angry.

'Ask him what he's so cross about,' said Alice.

'I don't speak budgerigar,' said Elvira. 'None of us do.'

So Alice took George's cage down from the dark corner in the kitchen and put it on the table by the window in her bedroom. She cleaned everything and gave George a new piece of cuttlefish and a red plastic mirror.

This is more like it, he thought.

Alice brought him fresh fruit every day and taught him all the rude words she knew. George had never been so happy.

'Who's a pretty boy?' he said to his reflection.

'Who's a pretty boy?' said the reflection.

'Both of us,' said George.

'Both of us,' said the reflection.

And both of them lived happily ever after, because all George had ever really wanted was someone to talk to, and a nice bit of cuttlefish, and a nice seat by the window.

SNAKE MAN

BY DIANNE BATES

'There's a new resident,' says Matron.
'His name is Mr Humphries and I'm sure
you'll like him.'

Amal, Gavin and I are working to get
our service badges for Scouts, so we visit
the old codgers at the retirement home
every second Saturday. It's pretty boring.
The olds talk about the same thing most
of the time – what it was like when they
were young. Really interesting. Not!
Or they clam up and we have to make
conversation with them, which is painful,
believe me.

But we soon discover this new guy is different.

'Call me Fred,' he says. 'Fearless Fred, that's me.'

The first thing he does is show off his wooden leg.

He taps it and winks at us. 'Got Woody here when a snake bit me.'

'A snake?' says Gavin, doubtfully. 'It must have been a whopper to bite off your leg.'

'Didn't exactly bite it off. It was a rare species of Asian water snake. Monster, it was.' Fred leans forward. 'Almost as big as the anacondas I used to wrestle with in South America.'

Gavin smirks, not believing a word of it. I feel the same way. This Fred is probably like my grandpa — full of tall stories.

Amal's a year younger than us – not as grown-up. It's easy to see he's fallen for the snake story, big time.

'Did you really fight with an anaconda, Fred?' he asks.

'Many a time, lad! Forty years I worked with snakes. Snake Man, that's what they called me. They said I even looked like a snake! Ha!'

He bares his yellowy teeth and chuckles at the thought.

'I think I'm better-looking than that – don't you?'

'Yeah,' says Gavin. 'A bit.'

Fred glares. 'Full of compliments, you are.'

'Tell us about the snakes,' says Amal, eagerly.

The old man settles back in the bed and closes his eyes. 'Right, lad! Love to . . . You know the reptile park outside town?'

Of course we do. We've been to the park on a school excursion.

'That was my baby.' Fred smiles proudly. 'I started it, ran the whole show for years.'

'Is this really true?' says Gavin.

Fred puts his right hand over his heart. 'May I be bitten by a tiger snake in my bed if I'm telling lies, son.'

'I could have told you that,' Amal says to Gavin.

'Most of the reptiles in that park I caught myself,' continues Fred. 'Crocs, alligators, giant turtles – a truckload of snakes . . .'

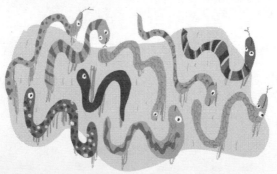

We listen agog to Fred as he launches into the story of his life as the Snake Man. He explains how to catch a croc, how to milk a snake for its serum, how crocs are meaner than alligators . . . He knows so much stuff that I start to think I was wrong. Maybe these aren't tall tales.

'But snakes are the meanest,' says Fred.

'Tell us about the snake that bit your leg,' I ask.

Fred chuckles again. 'Thought you'd never ask! I was knee-deep in swamp water. And from out of nowhere – *Wham! Bam!* It grabbed me. Teeth like razors. Grip like a vice. Wouldn't let go. Me screaming my lungs out.'

'What did you do?' says Gavin.

'The only thing I could do. Couldn't budge its head, so I hacked off its body.'

We all gasp.

'You mean its head still had hold of you?' I say.

'You got the picture, son. Just imagine it. I was in the jungle, delirious with fever, writhing in pain. Then I got lost. Nearly died, I did. All that time the rotten head was stuck hard onto my leg! And I do mean rotten. Phew! It was three days before I found help. At last, a doctor cut away the head. Of course, by then the gangrene had set in. My leg was a mass of . . . Well, you don't want to hear about that.'

'Yes, we do!' says Amal. 'Tell us!'

'No! Let's just say the leg was history. They sliced it off and gave me this chunk of wood.'

He taps the leg again. It makes a hollow sound, like a drum.

We listen for hours, but it seems like minutes. Fred can sure tell a good story.

Then he beckons us closer. 'You're nice kids,' he says as we huddle around him. 'I'd like to do you a good turn.'

'That'd be great,' says Amal.

Fred waves his finger at us. 'But you've got to prove yourselves! Think you're brave, do you, lads?'

We nod. Sure, we're brave.

'Then let me tell you about the treasure.'

'Treasure?' Amal's eyes shine brightly.

Gavin sighs. 'We're not little kids, you know. I believed you up until now, but treasure? Come on!'

Fred ignores him. 'I buried it just a few months ago, in the middle of the reptile park,' he whispers. 'In the komodo dragon pen.'

'What is this treasure?' I ask.

Fred shakes his head. 'That's for you to find out. All I can say is that it's in a metal box buried under the log near the waterhole. If you want it, lads, go get it.'

———

On the way home we talk about the treasure.

'He's probably made a fortune running that park,' I say. 'I bet the box is full of money.'

'Maybe it's got snakes in it,' Amal suggests.

'Don't be dumb,' snarls Gavin. 'If it did have snakes in it, they'd all be dead and rotten by now.'

Amal nods.

'Anyway, I don't believe a word he's told us,' says Gavin. 'All that stuff about the snake's head, losing his leg and then about the treasure? No way!'

'Well, how did he get his wooden leg then?' I say.

'Somebody pulled it off. The way he's pulling our legs.'

'I reckon we should check it out,' Amal says. 'It shouldn't be too hard to find out whether he's telling the truth or not.'

I think it probably is a big lie, but I'm not entirely sure. And there is a possible treasure at stake. That's what I tell Gavin.

'You're both mad,' he says.

Amal knows just how to answer that. 'Are you too scared to go into the komodo dragon pen, Gavin?' he asks.

'That settles it!' says Gavin. 'We're going! I'm not scared of stupid dragons.'

'And there might be treasure,' I say to cheer him up.

'Yeah,' he says begrudgingly. 'Maybe.'

———

That night we meet at the entrance to the park. We tell our parents we'll be home by seven. We never get into trouble, so they trust us.

But we don't mention anything about dragons.

It's dark, but there's a half-moon to guide us. Also, we've remembered to bring torches. Amal has a spade. I have rope.

We climb the wall. Easy. We're in.

The reptile park looks different at night.

'It's spooky,' Amal whispers.

'Don't be a wimp,' says Gavin.

Guided by our torches, we walk in single file along the well-marked paths. Somewhere a dog barks. I expect it to come flying out at us any second.

We pass the crocodile enclosure, the snake house . . .

'Did I ever tell you guys how I caught scarlet fever from a hippo?' Amal says.

'Not now!' I hiss.

Soon we're at the komodo dragon pen, enclosed by a low corrugated-iron fence. We flash our torches and locate three dragons on the other side of the pen. They stand, still as rocks. Their eyes stare at us, blood-red.

'They look ferocious.' For the first time Gavin sounds scared.

The dragons have long necks, strong legs and powerful tails. They're pretty big.

'I've heard they're fast runners,' Amal says. 'And they can eat big animals — swallow them in one gulp — even *people*.'

'Not now!' I hiss again.

I push Amal forward and we both tumble over the fence.

Gavin's right behind us. He's holding a jar. 'It's my little brother's insect collection,' he says. He shakes the jar. It's half-full of cockroaches, ants, flies, spiders and a couple of snails. 'You two keep watch. If the dragons get nasty, feed them.'

'You're kidding,' I say.

'Don't worry,' says Amal, crouching into a fighting stance. 'I've been learning judo for nearly a month now.'

For some reason that doesn't make me feel very confident.

The dragons watch our every move.

There's only one log near the waterhole. Gavin gets to work. He's only been digging for a few minutes when the spade hits metal.

'It's Fred's treasure!' he cries.

We all pull at what turns out to be an old biscuit tin with a lock on it.

'Quick! Open it!' says Amal.

I bash the spade hard against the lock. It springs open.

Gavin tips the tin upside down. All that falls out is a handwritten note.

'Well done!' it says. 'Bring this note back to me and I'll give you the treasure.'

I kick the tin angrily. 'What a rip-off!'

'Told you, didn't I?' says Gavin.

The dragons move closer.

'They're getting too friendly,' says Amal.

We run for the fence and clamber back to safety.

———

It's four o'clock the next day, visiting time at the retirement home.

'Come on,' says Gavin. 'I want to tell Fred what I think of him.'

'Me too,' I say.

Amal holds up the note. 'But what about the treasure? It says here that —'

Gavin stops him. 'Don't you get it? It was a joke! A dumb joke and we fell for it.'

'We'll see,' says Amal.

————

We find Fred with a huge smile on his face. 'You did it, didn't you?' he says. 'I can tell! You climbed into the den of the fierce komodo dragon! Am I right?'

'Yes,' says Gavin sourly. 'And all we got for our troubles was this piece of paper. There never was a treasure, was there?'

Fred looks hurt. 'Of course there's a treasure. I've guarded it carefully all my life. But now it's time to let it go. I tested you and you passed. The treasure is all yours!'

He undoes his wooden leg. It's hollow. Then he reaches in and pulls out a head – a shrivelled, gleaming snake's head!

'This is the head that took my leg!' he shouts. 'My most prized possession! My treasure!'

'Gee, thanks,' says Amal. 'I've never had one of those before.'

50 CENTS

BY GEORGE IVANOFF

It was round. It was made of silver.
It was very old. It was given to Alex by
his grandfather.

And it was gone!

His fifty-cent coin. His *special* fifty-cent
coin.

Alex sat at his desk in the empty
classroom, his head in his hands. He stared
at the old wooden box with the coins.
They were all there, except for that one
special coin. And he would gladly trade
them all for it.

He sighed and wondered what he was going to tell his grandfather. How could he explain that it was all because of an essay?

———

My Most Prized Possession
by Alex Kasoulis

My most prized possession is my coin collection. I have sixteen coins so far. They are all Australian coins. I only collect Australian ones because Australia is my country.

I don't collect ordinary coins. I spend them. I collect old coins – the sort they don't make anymore. Like one-cent and two-cent coins. They stopped making two-cent coins in 1989 and one-cent coins in 1990. That was before I was born.

I have a whole bunch of special
one-dollar coins with different designs.
They're called commemorative coins.
They're made for special occasions.
I have a 1988 First Fleet Bicentenary one,
a 1992 Barcelona Olympic Games one, a
1999 Year of Older Persons one, and
a 2001 Centenary of Federation one.
My favourite is the 2006 50 Years of
Television one.

I also have one coin from before
decimal currency. It's a penny from 1960.
A penny is sort of like one cent.

The very first coin I got was a 1966
fifty-cent coin. That's the year in which
decimal currency first started in Australia.
The coin is round, not like the dodecagon
we have today. It's still got the Australian
coat of arms on the *tails* side. But on the

heads side, the Queen looks a lot younger than on today's coins. It's really made of silver (with a bit of copper mixed in), not like today's fifty-cent coins that don't have any silver in them at all (they're a mix of copper and nickel).

My grandfather gave it to me. It's a very special coin. It's the first Australian money he ever had. He's told me the story lots of times. I can picture it in my head.

He found it when he came to Australia from Greece. He stepped off the ship. He looked around at his new country, then he looked down at the ground and there it was. It was shiny and new back then. He kept it in his pocket for forty-seven years. He never spent it. He said it brought him luck. He gave it to me for my birthday this year.

And that's how I started collecting coins.

———

Alex's teacher, Ms Ling, liked the essay. She liked it so much that she asked Alex if he could bring the coin collection to class so that everyone could see it. So, the very next day, Alex did.

He stood up at the front of the class and showed them his box of coins. He held them up, one by one, and told the class about each one – when they were made and how he got them. After he finished talking, Ms Ling got all the kids to line up so they could take a closer look at the coins.

It was great! Everyone liked the coins. Well, almost everyone.

As Alex returned to his seat, he saw Brad shaking his head. Brad sat behind him in class. He was bigger than Alex and he always seemed to be complaining about something.

'It's stupid,' said Brad. 'What's the point of having coins if you don't spend them?'

'You can't spend them,' Alex tried to explain. 'They're not used anymore. Anyway, I like having them. I don't want to lose them.'

'Lose them?' Brad laughed. 'You're the loser for collecting them.'

Brad reached into his pocket and pulled out a handful of coins.

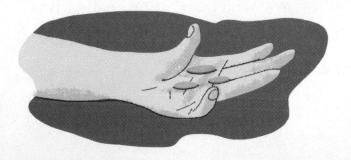

'These are better,' he said. 'I can spend these. And I'm going to spend them at lunchtime.'

Just then, the lunch bell rang.

'Class dismissed,' called out Ms Ling.

All the kids sprang to their feet and rushed for the door. In the confusion, Brad collided with Alex.

Coins went everywhere.

'Look what you made me do,' grumbled Brad, looking at the coins all over the floor.

'You'd better pick them up and sort them out,' Ms Ling said to the two boys. 'I don't think either of you want to lose any of your coins.'

'I know which are mine,' called Brad, bending down and scooping up a handful of coins.

Before Alex or the teacher could say anything, Brad and his handful of coins were out the door.

'Wait!' Ms Ling called out after him, but it was too late. He was gone.

Ms Ling sighed, shaking her head, then walked across the room to Alex. With her help, Alex picked up all of the coins and carefully sorted through them.

'Looks like they're all here,' said Ms Ling. She smiled at Alex and walked over to her office. 'Now, you'd better go off and have your lunch,' she called over her shoulder as she disappeared inside.

Alex breathed a sigh of relief and looked down at his prized coin collection. And then something caught his eye . . . something that didn't look right . . .

something that should have been round
. . . but wasn't.

Alex reached into the box and pulled
out his fifty-cent coin. Except, it wasn't
round. It had twelve sides.

Alex closed the box and ran out of
the classroom. He ran across the school
grounds towards the canteen. He arrived,
out of breath, just in time to see Brad
leaving the canteen with a chocolate bar
in his hand.

'Hey! Let me see your coins!' Alex
demanded between breaths.

'Why?' Brad asked suspiciously. He
reached into his pocket and pulled out a
tightly closed fist. 'You can't have any of
them, okay? They're for spending, not
collecting.'

Brad cautiously opened his hand to display the coins. He watched Alex carefully, ready to shut his hand and whisk the coins away if it looked like Alex wanted to take them.

Alex's heart sank. There were only three coins in Brad's hand – two twenty-cent coins and a dollar coin.

'Did you just spend a fifty-cent coin?' demanded Alex, desperation in his voice.

'Ahh.' Brad put the coins back in his pocket and took a step away from Alex. 'Dunno. Maybe.'

Alex suddenly pushed past him and ran to the side door of the canteen.

'Watch it,' Brad called after him.

Alex wasn't listening – he was too busy banging on the door.

The door opened suddenly, to reveal a very annoyed-looking woman. Her hair was a mess, her apron was covered in tomato sauce stains, and she looked like she was ready to hit something.

'Stand in line out the front, like the rest of the kids,' snarled the woman.

'I don't want to buy anything,' said Alex. 'I want my fifty cents back.'

'What?' asked the woman, her anger turning to confusion.

Alex took a deep breath to calm himself and explained what had happened.

———

It took Alex a whole hour to sort through all the coins in the canteen. Ms Ling gave him permission to continue searching through his afternoon classes. But no luck.

There were only ordinary, twelve-sided fifty-cent coins in the canteen.

'It's got to be here,' whimpered Alex, as he started sorting through the coins all over again.

'I hate to tell you this,' said the canteen lady, looking over his shoulder, 'but we give out an awful lot of change. Your coin could be with any of a hundred kids.'

———

Alex waited nervously in the principal's office. It had been ages since the principal, Mr Waylan, had made the announcement about the coin over the PA system. He had asked everyone who had been to the canteen that day to check their pockets for the coin. If anyone found it, they were asked to bring it to the principal's office.

So far, no one had shown up.

Alex paced up and down the office as he waited. As each minute ticked by, he grew more anxious. Someone had to have his coin!

There was a knock at the door, and Alex looked towards it hopefully.

Mr Waylan smiled at Alex and strode across the office to open the door. A young girl stood there, eyes wide with fear.

Alex's face lit up. Had this girl found his coin? Was she here to return it to him?

'Yes?' said Mr Waylan.

'Um . . . Ms Winston sent me,' said the girl, with a quavering voice. 'Um . . . to collect the flyers for the school fete.'

Alex felt a lump rise in his throat. He swallowed hard to get rid of it.

'Of course,' said Mr Waylan. 'Hold on a moment.'

He looked at his watch and turned to Alex.

'It's almost home time,' he said. 'If anyone had found the coin, they would have handed it in by now.'

Alex looked down at the floor sadly. He didn't want to leave. He didn't want to give up hope.

'I'm sorry. I think you should go back to class.' Mr Waylan turned to pick up the flyers from his desk. 'If anyone hands the coin in, I'll let you know.'

Alex returned to his classroom just as the end-of-school bell sounded. The other kids all pushed past him in their rush to escape school.

'Money is meant for spending,' chuckled Brad as he went past.

'I'm really sorry, Alex,' said Ms Ling. 'If I hadn't asked you to bring the coins . . .'

'It's okay,' Alex said sadly. 'Can I have another look around the room before I go?'

'Sure,' said his teacher. 'Take as long as you like. I'll be in my office if you need me.'

Alex crawled around on his hands and knees for ages. Finally, he gave up and slumped into the chair behind his desk, with his head in his hands.

His grandfather had carried the coin for forty-seven years and never spent it. Alex had it for only a few months and now it was gone. Spent at the school canteen.

Tears stung his eyes. He wiped them away angrily as he put the coin box into his schoolbag. He slung the bag over his shoulder and dragged his feet to the door. He stepped out into the bright sunlight and squinted. Looking around him, he saw kids running around and playing and being collected by their parents. He doubted that any of them would understand why it was so important to him. He sighed and looked down at his feet.

And there it was. Round and tarnished and . . . amazing! It must have rolled out of the classroom when it was dropped with all those other coins.

Alex crouched down to pick it up.
He had never felt as happy as he did that
moment. With the coin in his hand, he
stood up and looked at the world around
him. He felt the coin and thought that he
now understood how his grandfather must
have felt forty-seven years earlier.

Alex shoved the coin into his pocket
and went off to live the rest of his life in
the country his grandfather had chosen
as home. It was a country that used to
have round fifty-cent coins, but now had
twelve-sided ones instead. It was the
country in which he and his family lived.
It was the country that Alex proudly called
his country.

SIX LEGS, THREE HEADS

BY JENNY BLACKFORD

The alien had six legs and three heads and
long grey-blue fur, almost the same colour
as my oldest pair of blue jeans, the ones
Mum always wants to throw out. Lexie and
I just stared at it for a few minutes after
it appeared. Was it real, or had we been
playing handball too long in the afternoon
sun? School was over, but the playground
was still hot as a barbecue grill.

There were kids kicking balls and
yelling over on the sports field and the

teachers were around somewhere,
but Lexie and I had been playing handball
against the old brick wall for so long that
everyone had lost interest. We were the
only ones close enough to see the alien —
if it *was* an alien.

But then it started to talk to us.

'Take me to your uncle,' it said, and
waggled a couple of its twelve ears — or
the things that looked like ears — stuck
here and there all over its heads. It had four
ear-thingies on each head, which made it
look fairly odd, with its six legs and
blue-jeans fur and everything. There were
some tentacles as well, but every time
I tried to count them I got to five before
some of them moved, and I lost track.

Lexie and I stared at the alien for a
minute and walked a bit closer.

Lexie looked pretty silly with her mouth
wide open, despite her big green eyes and
long brown hair. Then I realised that my
own mouth was open too, and I closed it.

'What?' I said to the alien, as I'm
always a quick thinker under stress.

'Sorry, I forgot,' it said. 'Take me to
your uncle, *please.*'

The alien's tentacles shimmered in and
out of view. It seemed to be waiting for
one of us to say something.

I couldn't imagine anyone wanting to talk to my Uncle Nick, especially after what had happened with Dad's ride-on lawnmower last year. But Lexie has so many uncles that one of them might be interesting enough for an alien to visit.

'Uncle Braydon or Uncle Jayden or Uncle Jarrod or —' Lexie said.

Luckily, the alien interrupted her. 'Sorry, "uncle" is the wrong word,' it said.

'Did you mean "aunt"?' asked Lexie. I could easily imagine an alien wanting to meet her Aunty Madison. She's seriously interesting. Not many aunties teach karate and write video games.

'Actually, no! Not "aunt", either. It's tricky . . .' The alien was holding something in one of its tentacles — something that looked like a purple banana with lots of silver knobs. It pointed the purple banana at us and pressed one of the buttons.

For a moment I froze in fear. Then I pushed in front of Lexie but she shoved me aside and stood next to me.

The alien put the banana-shaped weapon up to one of its heads and spoke into it, and seemed to listen for an answer. It lowered the weapon and said to us, 'Take me to your "leader", please.'

Oh. The weapon was a translator.

But what should we tell the alien?

Lexie gave me a meaningful look and I looked back at her. Her big, green eyes were very wide. '"Leader",' she mouthed silently.

I knew what she meant. When this happens on TV, it means the aliens are going to invade Earth.

Before I could think of anything sensible to say, she turned to the alien and said, 'Why? And who are you?'

'My name is Zorkblap-bleep.' (Or, at least, that's what it sounded like to us.) 'I am a representative of the ancient and powerful race of Krelnnn. We have come to conquer your puny little planet.'

Uh-oh. The aliens really *were* here to invade Earth.

The alien was still talking away. 'We have a huge invasion force stationed on the next planet out,' it said. 'I believe you call it Mars. Resistance is futile.'

I took a deep breath. 'Why are *you* here, if the rest of your people are on Mars?' I said. 'And why have you come to our schoolyard?'

It's weird, but neither of us was really scared. Maybe it was just the soft blue-jeans-coloured fur. We *should* have been scared, of course. Any alien who's been beamed down onto Earth must have some pretty special technology backing it up.

'Schoolyard?' Zorkblap-bleep replied. 'A place for young Earthlings to play during the years when they are being educated in a communal manner?'

I thought for a minute. 'Yes, that's what this is,' I said, and pointed all around at the basketball hoops and the monkey bars and everything.

The alien's furry ears waggled madly. 'You mean this is not your Global Government? I am not in the right place?'

'Um, no. It should be obvious to you.'

I tried to think, fast. An alien was looking for our Global Government as a start to conquering Earth. I breathed deeply for a moment and gave the alien a quick run-down on the difference between an inner-city Aussie primary school and a Global Government – including the fact that there is no Global Government on Earth, yet. Or maybe ever, the way the politicians are going.

'So,' I finished up, 'why do you want to conquer Earth anyway?'

Its ears wriggled, presumably expressing some mysterious alien emotion or other. 'Actually, I'm not sure. I'm the exotic language expert, not one of the military. I wanted them to send someone else down with me, but they were all busy on Mars.'

I said, 'You don't know *why* you're trying to conquer Earth?'

'No,' it replied. 'The climate on Mars is so much better. A resort there would be delightful! Those cool low-oxygen breezes in the twilight – so relaxing. The dust is so good for the fur. And such a lovely view of Saturn and Jupiter by night.'

I had no idea what to say to that. Luckily, the alien language expert just loved to talk.

'Do you think that conquering Earth is a bad idea, then?'

Lexie and I looked at one another. Yes, it was definitely a bad idea, but how were we going to convince him?

She stood up very straight. She said to it, 'If you're the exotic languages expert, I guess you think we're pretty exotic.'

'Oh, yes,' it said. 'You humans are fabulously rare and fascinating. Bipeds! Amazing! How do you balance with only two legs? We watch nature documentaries about you for hours. And we just love your films and TV, especially the science fiction.'

If this had been a cartoon, a little light bulb would have come on over Lexie's head. She winked at me and made her face serious as she turned back to the alien.

'If you've seen a lot of our science fiction movies, you should have some idea what we exotic bipeds would think about blue alien overlords,' she said.

'Oh,' it said worriedly, if you can imagine a blue alien sounding worried. 'Like *Mars Attacks*.'

In a firm tone, Lexie continued. 'We would rather destroy the whole planet than submit. And we would keep on fighting forever, until we found some way to win. Zorkblap-bleep, do you remember *Independence Day?*'

It nodded two of its heads. The other one looked undecided.

Lexie clearly has a great future ahead of her as a diplomat one day. 'Even if you win, Earth will be a total mess. No one will be able to make any new movies or TV shows. There won't be any more Terminator movies. And no more Doctor Who.'

'No more Doctor Who?' Zorkblap said, waggling its ears madly. 'That's terrible! I give in. But how can I convince the soldiers? They're determined to conquer this planet.'

Lexie put on her best serious look – the one she uses when she asks hard questions in class. 'My Aunty Madison swore me to secrecy, but maybe it would be in the best interests of Earth if I tell you about the Anti-Matter Planet Destructor that she designed.'

Wow! Lexie's aunt was even more interesting than I'd thought!

'Please tell me, young Earthling,' Zorkblap-bleep replied. 'I must stop the Krelnnn from destroying Earth! Life on Krelnnnar would not be worth living without Earthling science fiction! Please give me a reason that I can explain to them.'

'Deep inside the deepest mountain,' Lexie said, 'there's a secret cave of ice, invisible to radar or any other form of scientific detection. Only Aunty Madison knows where it is. Inside it, miraculously suspended from the icy roof, there are two giant gems as big as elephants: a huge red ruby, and a green anti-ruby just as huge. They're this far apart.'

She held her two hands out, so close that I could barely see sunlight between them.

'If they ever touch, the whole Earth will explode, and the blast will be so huge that it will destroy Mars as well.'

She pointed at Zorkblap-bleep. 'The only thing that keeps the ruby and the anti-ruby apart, and stops Earth being blown to tiny pieces, is the force of my aunt Madison's mind. She has to concentrate on them all day and all night, even when she's asleep. And she's not afraid to use it! If she stops for even a moment . . .' Lexie shuddered theatrically. 'Boom!'

Zorkblap-bleep was shivering with fear. I have to admit, I was worried too. What if Lexie's Aunty Madison got distracted one day?

Zorkblap-bleep said, 'I will return to the mother ship and explain everything to my leaders. We will not try to conquer Earth. You have proven that it is just not worth it.'

Lexie and I agreed vigorously.

'And I will keep your secret,' it said. 'I am honoured that you trusted me with it.'

Lexie blushed and nodded.

Zorkblap-bleep walked back a few steps, waggled the purple banana at us cheerfully, and blinked out of sight.

'Phew,' I said to Lexie. 'Well done! You were amazing.'

'It was nothing,' she said, but she went pink. I think she was pleased.

I couldn't help asking. I had to know. 'Is it true? About the ruby and the anti-ruby?'

'Kind of,' Lexie said, looking a bit embarrassed. 'It was in a video game that Aunty Madison designed.' She giggled and I started to laugh, and couldn't stop. Soon, she was laughing like a mad thing too, with tears running down her cheeks. Every time I managed to stop, she said, 'Video game,' and I started laughing again.

When she stopped, I said, 'Anti-Matter Planet Destructor,' and that started her off again. And when we finally both ran out of puff and I caught my breath, I said, 'There's no point telling our parents about this, is there?'

'No,' she said, panting slightly. 'Or anybody else, for that matter.'

That was a relief. Nobody would ever have believed us.

So we went back to the still-warm brick wall, chuckling now and then, and played handball for a while, as if it was a perfectly ordinary afternoon after school.

That was three months ago, and we've never talked about how we saved Earth from destruction by an ancient and powerful race of aliens. But just occasionally, Lexie catches my eye and holds her hands close together, like the giant ruby and the anti-ruby almost touching one another, and we both double over, helplessly laughing and laughing.

PEDRO AND THE PERILOUS PAINTBRUSH

BY KERRI LANE

Dear reader: This is the first time these words have ever been put on paper. Up until now, only three people knew all the facts of this story. And one of them has disappeared ... When you've read this you, too, will know the truth. You will know the secret of the Perilous Paintbrush.

It was Art Day, and the minute the new art teacher walked into the classroom I knew

I was in trouble. The last time I'd seen her she'd been covered in my breakfast . . .

We were late because my baby sister had been upset all night, and I'd had to eat breakfast on the run. Looking back, maybe muesli with yoghurt and mashed banana might not have been the best choice to eat while you're walking along, but that didn't make it my fault.

The lady had cannoned straight into mc in the playground! And then she'd screeched at me in the scariest voice I'd ever heard. It was a cross between a crow's call and a train whistle! I'd tried telling her I was sorry, and I'd even tried to help her clean up the mess, but she'd just pushed me away and kept screeching.

Now here she was, and those beady eyes had found me.

'I'm Miss Zelda,' she said as she handed out brushes and paint.

When she finally reached my table her long, pointy nose quivered, just like a rat's nose quivers. Her small, black eyes glittered like lumps of hard coal. 'What's your name?' she demanded.

'Um, Pedro,' I answered in a shaky voice.

Her eyes narrowed to slits. 'Well, *"Um Pedro"*, I think this brush would be the best one for you.' Her voice was different now. It was low and sly as she continued. 'It's special. It belonged to a famous painter named Vincent van Gogh.'

The brush was old and had hardly any bristles left. Worse than that, it looked like it would break if I even breathed on it. My heart sank.

'Children,' she began, 'we're going to concentrate on portraits today. A portrait is a painting of a person.'

She gave us some tips and then told us to begin by painting a picture of *her*. She kept staring at me, and I couldn't think straight. Everyone else was working, so I took a deep breath and hoped for the best.

But as soon as I dipped the brush into the paint, something strange happened. The brush began to hum, and then it just started moving by itself! My hands could hardly keep up. It didn't seem to need paint, it was able to change colour whenever it wanted.

The strokes were bold and fast, and in minutes I had a portrait. But it was awful! The woman in the picture had Miss Zelda's face as well as rat's ears and whiskers!

I tried to hide it but, within seconds, Miss Zelda had pounced on me. In that shrieking voice, she was yelling for Mr Mason, the principal.

'Pedro!' he bellowed after seeing the painting. 'This is a disgrace! Apologise this instant!'

'But, Mr Mason, I didn't do it! It's the brush! It's . . . it's . . . it's magic!'

Mr Mason shook his head. 'I can't believe you'd tell such stories, Pedro. You've always been such a sensible boy. I'm very disappointed in you.'

As he walked away, everyone stared at me. I didn't know what to do. It wasn't my brush! I had to get a new one. But as I picked it up to give it to Miss Zelda, it began to hum again. Suddenly, it was working on the fresh paper on my desk. And just like before, it moved so quickly I could barely keep up. When it was finished my eyes almost popped out of my head. I think I yelped, because Mr Mason stopped and came back.

'Pedro!' His voice sounded angry, and with good reason. It was a portrait of him with long fangs, huge pointy pixie ears and an enormous nose with a wart on the end.

'But, Mr Mason,' I pleaded. 'I truly didn't do it! It's the brush! I can't draw that well. Honest!'

'You think this is *good*?' he asked in an amazed voice. 'You're a very rude young

man! Go to the library and wait until
I come for you.'

Slowly, I trudged out of the room,
still unable to believe what had happened.
My friends looked shocked, some looked
worried. One face, though, had a sly grin.
Miss Zelda! She was punishing me! But
how? Was *she* magic too?

In the library, I sat in a quiet corner
and tried to think. Who did Miss Zelda
say had owned the brush? Van Go?
Van Goff? Maybe if I looked him up,
I might be able to work it out. The
computer was off-limits, so I grabbed
an encyclopedia and found a name.
Vincent van Gogh!

Okay, so what I found out was that he's
really famous *now*, but he only sold one
painting when he was alive. And that he

really liked painting flowers best. But how would that help me?

'If only I could convince Mr Mason that Miss Zelda is behind this!' I muttered to myself.

As soon as the words left my mouth, I felt a warm buzzing feeling against my back. The brush! Oh, no! I pulled it out of my back pocket.

The brush was going crazy – worse than before. It was shaking and twirling and humming so loudly I was sure the librarian would hear. I darted into the hallway. The brush wanted to paint, but thankfully there was no blank paper around. But there were big bare WALLS, and the brush was dragging me towards them! *Oh no!*

I fought back. I tried to pull my arm away from the wall. I tried shoving my hand in my pocket. I tried to shake the brush out of my hand, but nothing worked! That brush was like a magnet being drawn to those walls.

As soon as it made contact, pictures of cats, dogs, monkeys and donkeys appeared. All kinds of animals – and they all had Miss Zelda's face!

'No! Stop!' I yelled, but this time the brush was crazier than ever. Faster and faster it went.

'Stop that right now!' a deep voice boomed.

'I'm trying, Mr Mason! Please help me!' I yelled back.

With a grunt, Mr Mason's big hand grabbed mine. 'I said stop that . . . Oh dear! Why isn't it stopping? Pedro? Why can't I let go?'

Our hands moved faster than the wind. I darted a quick glance at Mr Mason and his eyes were bigger than saucers. 'I tried to tell you!' I panted. 'It's the brush! I think it's magic and Miss Zelda is making it work.'

'That's nonsense,' said Miss Zelda, who had appeared in the hallway. 'He's just an evil boy who throws breakfast at people and disobeys orders. He should be punished severely!'

Suddenly, the brush stopped and we spun towards her voice. Our hands were still glued to the brush. And before we could stop it, that crazy brush lunged towards Miss Zelda. I heard myself gasp as it made contact. The brush was painting Miss Zelda's face! First a moustache! Then a pointy beard! Big fluffy eyebrows and a red clown's nose!

Mr Mason was spluttering, trying to apologise. But then the strangest thing happened. Miss Zelda began to disappear!

Her last words echoed around us. 'You can't do this to me! I stole you! You're mine!'

And then she was gone.

We couldn't believe our eyes. I think Mr Mason would have flopped onto the floor in shock if he could have, but the brush was still humming. He didn't seem to know what to do – which made two of us.

Then I had an idea.

'Mr Mason! Quick, help me turn back to the wall,' I urged.

Together, we heaved, pulling the brush towards the wall.

'Now, we have to yell "flowers". Ready? One, two, three: FLOWERS!'

As soon as the word left our mouths, the brush grew still. Slowly, it began to paint beautiful flowers over all the ugly faces. Pinks, purples, yellows and blues . . . It was amazing. But, best of all, we were able to loosen our grip on the brush handle.

'I think we might be able to put it down now,' I whispered.

And the brush was finally still.

'How did you do that?' Mr Mason asked.

I shrugged my shoulders. 'It was a guess. Mr Van Gogh liked painting flowers best, and maybe Miss Zelda made the brush paint other stuff it hated and it got really mad.'

'Well, I owe you an apology – several apologies – Pedro. Though I don't know how we're going to explain this to the rest of the school and to the parents.'

In the end, we didn't explain it. Mr Mason tried, but unless they'd seen it with their own eyes, nobody believed his story. They all thought it was a great joke. So, he gave up trying.

That is why I had to write it all down, so you'd know what *really* happened.

And if you ever get to visit Goodart Primary School and see the paintings on our hallway walls, you'll know that this story is true.

Oh, and by the way, you'll find the brush at the Great Museum of Art where we sent it that very day. But don't EVER try to pick it up.

MASSIVE MICK AND THE GREAT FROG RACE

BY MICHAEL PRYOR

My mate Phil never has enough money. That's why he's always coming up with crazy ideas for getting rich.

Most of his ideas are stupid, but some of them are *amazingly* stupid. Like his idea to make dog-hair jumpers. Have you ever seen a bald dog? Well, when Phil shaved his own dog, it made Bruiser look like a naked rat. And Bruiser's hair was useless for making into wool. I told Phil before he started that Bruiser was a sheepdog, not a sheep, but Phil usually ignored good advice. Phil's mum made him buy heaps of 15+ sunblock to stop Bruiser from getting sunburn, so the whole idea ended up *costing* Phil money.

At least he never got around to going ahead with his idea to recycle used tissues.

———

But that's why Phil had this crazy scheme for the Great Frog Race. 'It's simple!' he crowed. 'People love races! People love excitement! People love thrills!'

'Sure,' I said. 'But do people love frogs?'

'Don't worry about that,' he said confidently. 'By the time the Great Frog Race is finished, the whole town'll be jumping!'

We were in Phil's backyard, near
the wattle tree, trying to train Bruiser.
I put down the ball. It was no use trying
to do anything when Phil was on a roll.
Of course, as soon as I put the ball down,
Bruiser grabbed it and zoomed off into
the distance. Typical. At least his hair was
growing back. He now looked like a ball
of rusty steel wool on legs.

'Okay,' I said to Phil. 'How are you
going to make money out of this scheme?'

Phil waved his hand in the air. 'Simple.
I charge an entry fee, and after the prizes
are handed out, I have a nice profit. Don't
worry. It's all under control.'

I shuddered – I had heard those words
a thousand times, and I knew that Phil
was about as 'controlled' as a herd of
stampeding rhinos.

Phil's idea was to hold the Great Frog Race at the local Community Market. He thought the Scout Hall would be the perfect place for an All-Star Frog Race. *All-Star Disaster more like it*, I thought to myself.

The Scout Hall was a rundown sort of place. In fact, it made the local tip look like a desirable neighbourhood. The walls needed paint, and the roof leaked even when it wasn't raining.

'Isn't it great?' Phil said as he rubbed his hands together. 'Come on, let's get the track ready.'

We'd arrived early to set up. At least, that's what Phil said. It actually meant that I did all the work while Phil supervised. As I was banging in nails and carrying wood in from outside, he kept telling me what was going on in the rest of the hall.

'Hey, you should see all the cake boxes! Look, *see*, stacked almost up to the ceiling! You know what that means. Phwooar!'

Phil loved cakes, and would happily eat a whole chocolate layer cake by himself. He used to tell me he had an allergy. An allergy to *not* eating chocolate cakes. The only cure was lots of chocolate cakes. I think he made that one up.

'Look,' he said. 'Mrs McFloon is having her Cat Show again! You think we should go and get Bruiser to help?' I shook my head, but Phil wasn't looking. 'Cats everywhere. Hey, what do you call a cat with a lemon in its mouth?'

'A sour puss,' I mumbled around a mouthful of nails. This was Phil's only joke, and I'd heard it a million times.

'A sour puss. Sour puss! Get it?'

At least *he* laughed.

I finally finished and wiped my hands. The track was about fifteen metres long, with six lanes marked out with coloured strings. 'Phil,' I said, 'how will they stick to their lanes?'

'Doesn't matter. We let 'em go at this end, and whoever gets to the other end first is the winner. Simple.'

'So is getting your head stuck in a recycled clothing bin.'

'My head *wasn't* stuck — I was just having a look around.' Phil turned away, and I had my first good look at the hall since it had filled up.

There were junk stalls and bookstalls and garden stalls, but most of the hall was taken up with the mega Cake Stall,

the Cat Show and our Great Frog Race
track. Mrs McFloon waved at us from the
benches of the Cat Show, while the ladies
at the Cake Stall looked nervously at the
piles of cake boxes stacked up behind
them.

Then the doors were opened to the
public.

Suddenly, Phil was buried under
people wanting to enter their frogs in the
Great Frog Race. They must have been
out all night, searching the creek and the
swamp. There were frogs in jars, frogs in
plastic containers, big frogs, little frogs,
green, brown and striped frogs. I left Phil
to deal with the entries, and I wandered

off to look at the rest of the Community Market.

I was examining a very interesting pair of furry dice when the entire hall suddenly went quiet. It reminded me of those times when the dentist walks into the packed waiting room. I turned and looked at the front doors.

There stood . . . Barry Burns, a battered cake box under his arm, an even more battered smirk across his mouth!

Now, I suppose that somewhere there is someone who thinks that Barry Burns is a lovely boy – probably the same sort of person who thinks that sharks are cute and Tasmanian devils are just a little bit grumpy. Let's face it, Barry Burns was a bully. And to make things worse, he was a *smart* bully. Now, most bullies are pretty

stupid. The old 'What's that behind you?'
trick used to work for me with most
bullies, but not with Barry. He'd never
turn around, so I could never run away.
He had a way of smiling that made a
crocodile look harmless, then BAM!

I shuddered. The only thing Barry
Burns liked better than bullying was
winning. And in the battered cake box
he was holding, I just knew there was
a frog he wanted to enter in the Great
Frog Race.

He rolled up to the table. 'Right,'
he growled. 'Here's the winner.' In front
of Phil's nose, Barry opened the box.
Inside was a monster.

Well, I suppose it only *looked* like a
monster. It filled the box, warts and all
(and it had plenty of warts, especially

around its enormous toady mouth), and it sat there staring at Phil as if to say, 'What are you looking at, fly-features?' It must have weighed ten kilos.

You've got to hand it to Phil. He was gutsy, at least where money was concerned. 'Sorry!' he grinned. 'No can do. It's not a frog. It's a cane toad.'

Barry blinked. 'So? Uncle Ratso sent it down from Queensland and I want to race him. Let's see if anyone objects.' He turned to the crowd that had gathered. 'Anyone have any problems with me entering Massive Mick in this race?'

There was silence for a second, and then he took a step forward. Cries of 'No worries!' and 'It's okay with me!' broke out, and Barry grinned.

'Let's go,' he grunted.

Phil shrugged and organised the heats to decide the finalists. Barry laughed when Phil asked when Massive Mick was going to race. 'In the final, mate. In the final, and not before.'

An hour later, Phil had narrowed the field down to five finalists. And Massive Mick. 'At last,' Barry said, and lifted the huge toad from the box. 'We'll take Lane Three.'

The other finalists looked like toys next to Massive Mick. Their owners held them nervously, waiting for the start. The crowd pressed around, some hanging from the rafters. There was a silence so thick you could cut it with a rolling pin.

Phil stood at the finish line, his mouth set in a grim line. 'Go!' he shouted, and the crowd erupted.

The five frogs leapt forward as soon as their owners let go, but then they stopped as they tried to remember exactly what they were supposed to do again. Massive Mick just sat there.

'Come on, you lazy lump!' Barry yelled, but Mick just looked at him.

'What's your problem, slimehead?' he seemed to be thinking.

The crowd whistled and cheered as the frog in Lane Six took two leaps in a row. Lane One tried to climb the wall, and Lanes Five and Four started wrestling. Mick just sat there.

Suddenly, the warty giant stretched a leg and seemed to yawn. It took one waddling jump and landed next to the two wrestling frogs.

And ate them.

The crowd went berserk. 'Hey! That's
not fair!' shouted one of the owners. Then
she noticed Barry looking at her. 'I mean,
er . . . I hope it was tasty.'

Massive Mick dragged himself around
the track, blundering through the lane
ribbons. One gulp, and the frog in

Lane One was gone. A hop, and Lane Two disappeared. Mick looked around, only to see the frog in Lane Six madly scrambling towards the finish.

Two thundering leaps and a heavy hop landed Massive Mick right in front of the frog. Mick opened his mouth, and the frog jumped straight in. Mick looked very pleased with himself.

The noise was deafening. The crowd was arguing, booing and cheering all at once. Phil was holding his head in his hands. Barry was looking like his toad.

I suppose all the noise was why no one heard Bruiser. He rammed through the crowd like a heat-seeking missile, knocking people over with his wagging tail. He saw Phil and started to go to him. Then Bruiser saw the toad.

For a split second, everything froze. The toad stared at Bruiser. Bruiser stared at the toad. The crowd stared at both of them. Then Bruiser bounded, snatched Massive Mick up and ran away.

I thought the roof was going to lift off. Barry shouted, 'Hey!' Phil yelled, 'Bruiser, drop it!', and the crowd roared with delight.

Bruiser scurried between legs and under tables. Phil chased him, and Barry chased Phil. Bruiser leapt over the Cake Stall, and the mountain of cake tins toppled, adding to the noise. People tried to catch Bruiser, but only got in the way. He was having a ball, and held Mick gently all the time.

It was only when Bruiser bowled Mrs McFloon over that he realised there were cats around. He dropped Mick, and then the real trouble started. It was like a tornado in a fur factory – with sound effects. Cats screamed everywhere, and Bruiser seemed to be in a hundred places at once. People ran for the doors or tried to help. Tables crashed and cake boxes were kicked up and down like ice-hockey pucks. It was great.

I sat up near the ceiling. From my perch on an old knot and splice display, I saw everything. It was like one of those old movies, with everything in fast motion. Cats were jumping on people's backs, trying to get away from the maniac dog. I thought I saw Mrs McFloon wearing a lumpy, furry hat, but it was just an overweight Siamese on top of her head. Barry was crawling around, looking for

Massive Mick. Phil was guarding his money.

When everything was calmer, I climbed down and went to Phil. 'That seemed to go pretty well,' I said. He gave a sickly grin.

We watched as everyone picked up their purchases – the books and plants and cake boxes that hadn't been trampled – and the hall began to empty. I didn't like the way people looked at Phil as they left, but I suppose he was used to that sort of thing.

'Where's Barry?' I asked.

'I lied. I said I saw the toad head down the drain. Barry was going to get a torch so I could go after it. I suppose I'll have to give all the money back, too,' he added sadly.

Eventually, we were the only ones left in the place. I packed up the racetrack and turned to leave. I picked up a last cardboard box. It was empty, but there was something strange about it. 'Phil?' I said, looking at the air holes in the battered lid. 'Is this yours?'

'I didn't buy a cake.'

We looked at it, then at each other.

'Are you thinking what I'm thinking?' I said.

'Uh-huh.' Phil shuddered. Somewhere out there, someone was going to put a cake box on the dinner table, ready to enjoy a passionfruit sponge or something. And when they opened it . . .

'You know,' said Phil, 'frogs were a lousy idea.'

'Really?' I said. Perhaps he was starting to see the light.

'Yeah. A *cat* race — now *that's* where the money is!'

COCKROACH

BY ANDY GRIFFITHS

'You know, there's a world of opportunity
out there,' says Mr Bainbridge. 'A world
full of opportunities, just waiting for
a young man like you. Yes, a world of
opportunities!'

'Yes, sir.'

I feel like taking the opportunity to tell
him to shut up, but I'm much too polite
for that. Besides, Mr Bainbridge is Dad's
boss.

I'm under strict instructions tonight
to just sit quietly, behave myself and not
muck up in any way. The worst thing is,

Dad has made me promise not to play any practical jokes.

No squirting flowers. No exploding cans of peanuts. No rubber vomit.

Dad said that if I tried any funny stuff at the dinner table, my pocket money would be stopped for a month.

I made the promise, but I don't think Dad realises how hard it is for me. See, the thing is, I'm a practical-joke-a-holic. I need to play practical jokes like other people need to breathe air and drink water.

I don't really see what's wrong with a few harmless practical jokes, anyway. They help to break the ice. It's not like I've got a lot to say to Mr and Mrs Bainbridge.

'Too many kids these days,' says Mr Bainbridge, 'expect opportunity to come to them. But it doesn't work that way. Oh, no. You've got to go out and grab it by the neck. When I was a young man –'

'Dinner is served!' says Mrs Bainbridge, coming into the room with an enormous bowl of salad.

'Thank God!' I blurt out, before I can stop myself.

'I beg your pardon?' says Mr Bainbridge.

'Um, I just meant, um, let us be thankful to God for such a beautiful spread,' I say quickly.

Mum and Dad are glaring at me.

'Oh,' says Mr Bainbridge, 'that's all right then. For a moment there I thought you were taking the Lord's name in vain. That's the other trouble with young people today. They have no –'

'Perhaps you'd like to say grace, Andy?' says Mrs Bainbridge. 'The lasagne is getting cold.'

'Oh, ah, yes,' I say.

It's been so long since I've said grace, I can barely remember the words.

Everybody closes their eyes.

For a moment I'm tempted to say, 'Two, four, six, eight – bog in, don't wait!' but then I remember Dad's warning.

'For what we are about to receive . . .'

I know I should have my eyes shut too, but somebody's got to keep theirs open to make sure that everyone else's stay closed. And, as I'm the one saying grace, it might as well be me.

But, as I'm trying to think of the next line, I see something in the salad bowl. Something oval. Something dark brown.

Something that looks a lot like a dead cockroach.

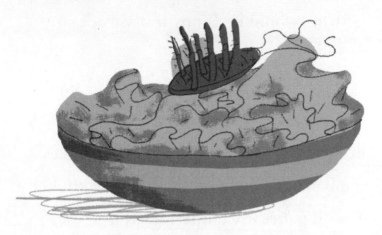

At least, I think it's dead. It's sort of hard to tell. All I know is, there's a cockroach in the salad, and it probably wasn't put there on purpose. Unless Mr and Mrs Bainbridge eat cockroaches – which seems unlikely. I mean, Mr Bainbridge must get paid more than Dad, and *we* don't have to eat cockroaches.

'May the Lord make us truly thankful . . .'

Truly thankful for a cockroach?

This would be funny if it wasn't so serious.

I can't just put up my hand and say, 'Excuse me, but there's a dead cockroach in the salad.' It would make it look like the Bainbridges have a really dirty kitchen. They'd get really embarrassed because they'd think that we think that cockroaches fall into their food all the time.

But even worse still, Dad might think that I put it there for a joke. And that would mean trouble.

I have to get it out before anybody notices. For everybody's sake.

I grab a spoon to scoop the roach off the salad leaf . . .

'Amen,' says Mr Bainbridge, finishing grace for me as he opens his eyes.

He picks up the salad bowl.

'Salad, Andy?'

'Yes, please,' I say. Luck is running my way.

Mr Bainbridge passes me the bowl. I scoop a large portion of salad onto my plate, including the top two pieces of lettuce with the dead roach in between.

So far so good.

Mrs Bainbridge places a large slab of lasagne on the other side of my plate. Normally my mouth would be watering, but the cockroach has kind of taken the edge off my appetite.

'Would you care for some potatoes, Andy?'

Mrs Bainbridge passes me a bowl full of steaming spuds. I pick out one and pass the bowl to Mr Bainbridge.

Now that the roach is on my plate, all I have to do is get it into my pocket before anybody notices.

But first I have to distract them.

'What a beautiful landscape!' I point to a painting on the wall above Mum's head.

Everybody turns to look.

I lift up the piece of lettuce. But the cockroach has other ideas.

It's not dead.

It jumps off the lettuce leaf onto the table and starts running.

Straight towards me.

The roach reaches the edge of the table and tumbles onto my lap. I try to

brush it onto the floor, but it disappears
underneath my napkin.

Luckily, the others are all still studying
the painting. Nobody else has seen the
roach's 30-centimetre sprint. I discreetly
lift the corner of my napkin to see where
the roach has got to, but it's not there.
I feel a gentle pricking on my stomach.
It's underneath my shirt!

I freeze. The roach crawls around my
side and onto my back.

I guess I could crush it by throwing
myself back, hard against the chair.
It would probably work, but it might take
more than one go to actually kill it and
this could give Mr and Mrs Bainbridge
the wrong impression. I don't want them
thinking I've lost my mind.

'Are you keen on painting, Andy?' asks Mrs Bainbridge.

'I like it,' I say, 'but I'm not very good at it.' I'm trying hard not to panic.

'Ah!' says Mr Bainbridge. 'But practice makes perfect! If a fellow really wants to do something badly enough and he's prepared to apply himself for long enough, then –'

'Yes, dear,' says Mrs Bainbridge. That's all very well, but perhaps Andy doesn't want to be a painter. What are your favourite subjects, Andy?'

I'm trying hard to concentrate on the conversation, but it's not easy. The roach has relocated itself underneath my left arm. I can hardly breathe. It feels like it's burrowing into my armpit.

'I guess I like English the best. Not too crazy about maths or science.'

'No, no, no!' says Mr Bainbridge.
'You don't want to neglect your maths
and science. Keep your options open,
that's what I say. Science and technology –
that's where the opportunities are.'

Mrs Bainbridge rolls her eyes.

I'd feel sorry for her if I wasn't feeling
so sorry for myself. I only have to put
up with him for one night. She has to live
with him.

The roach has finished playing in my
armpit and now I can feel it crawling
down my chest. I can't stand it anymore.

That damn roach could be laying eggs
in my belly button for all I know. They're
probably incubating in my stomach right
now. They'll hatch inside me and burst
out of my chest, like the face-hugger
in *Alien*.

I ask for directions to the toilet and excuse myself from the table.

It's roach-killing time.

The bathroom is upstairs. I lock the door behind me and yank off my T-shirt. It flies across the room, skims the top of the toilet bowl, and lands in a heap beside it. But the roach is not on my chest.

Or my back.

Uh-oh — not a moment to lose!

I kick my shoes off, and peel off my trousers and jocks in one swift movement.

I'm completely naked — except for my socks — but I still can't find the roach.

There are only two places it can be — one of which is too horrible to even think about.

I study the pile of clothes carefully.
The roach emerges from the bottom of
my jeans. It's creeping up the left leg.
I pick up one of my shoes. Very slowly – so
that the roach doesn't notice – and raise it
high above my head.

The roach reaches the bottom button
of my fly.

I take a deep breath.

But something holds me back. If
I smash it right there, I'm going to end
up with its pasty white guts splattered
all over the front of my jeans. Not cool.
Might look like I've had an embarrassing
accident. I put my shoe down slowly.
The roach crawls back inside my jeans.

There's got to be a better way than
splattering.

I look around for inspiration.

There's a window above the toilet. It's high and very small, but it might do. I could climb up there, hold the jeans outside the window and shake the cockroach off.

No sweat. No splatter. No roach.

I pick up the jeans, taking care to hold the waist and the trouser legs closed so that the roach can't escape. I shut the lid of the toilet and use it to step up onto the cistern. The window is now level with my head.

I lean against the wall for balance and slide the window open as far as it will go. I push the jeans out of the window and shake them as hard as I can.

Suddenly, the roach is on my hand. I get such a fright, I drop the jeans, lose my footing and crash down into the bath.

I feel like lying here, closing my eyes and pretending it's all just a bad dream — but I have to find the roach before it disappears again. I get out of the bath and study myself in the mirror.

The roach is sitting on top of my head.

This time I know exactly what to do. It's not going to be pleasant, but it's the only way. This is one tricky cockroach and I can't afford to take any chances.

I go back to the toilet and get down onto my knees. I lift the lid and bend lower and lower until my head is right inside the bowl.

Then I take a deep breath, reach up and push the flush button.

It's horrible.

Toilet water up my nose.

Toilet water in my ears.

Toilet water in my mouth.

Finally, the flushing stops. I sit back up.

It's gone.

But so are my jeans.

I can't go back to the table without them. What would I say? I can just imagine the conversation:

MRS BAINBRIDGE: Where are your pants, Andy?

ME: Oh, I accidentally dropped them out of the bathroom window, Mrs Bainbridge.

MR BAINBRIDGE: Isn't that annoying! It happens to me all the time. Why don't you have a look in my wardrobe and see if there's anything there that fits you?

Yeah, right. Dream on. Meanwhile, back in the real world, I'm naked from the waist down.

There's no choice, really, but to climb out the window and fetch my jeans. I don't fancy a month without pocket money.

I climb back on top of the cistern and lean across to the tiny window. It's going to be a tight squeeze, but since I haven't eaten any dinner yet, I reckon I'll make it.

I grip the narrow ledge and pull myself up and halfway out.

It's a long way to the ground. I didn't realise I was so high up.

But I'm in no danger of falling.

I'm stuck.

I can't go forward and I can't go back.

And to make matters worse, there's someone banging on the door.

'It's taken!' I yell.

'Is everything all right?' calls Mum. 'You've been in there an awfully long time!'

'Yes,' I call. 'I'll be out in a second.'

'He's not answering!' says Mum. 'I think there's something wrong!'

She can't hear me because my head is outside the house.

Then I hear Mr Bainbridge's voice.

'Stand back, everyone. I'm going to break the door down.'

Oh, great. My hero.

I hear a huge crash.

Mr Bainbridge is no muscle man, but the flimsy lock snaps like it's Arnie Schwarzenegger himself out there.

'Oh my God!' says Mr Bainbridge.

For probably the first time in his
life, Mr Bainbridge has taken the Lord's
name in vain, but I guess the last thing he
expected to see was my bare bum staring
at him from his bathroom window.

'Oh my God!' says Mrs Bainbridge.

'Oh my God!' says Mum.

'Oh my God!' says Dad.

'I know this seems a little unusual,'
I yell, 'but there's a perfectly reasonable
and logical explanation! See, while I was
saying grace, I saw this cockroach in
the salad bowl, only I didn't want to say
anything because . . .'

But I might as well be telling it to the
man in the moon.

Mum and Dad and the Bainbridges
are too busy gabbling on about ladders
and fire brigades and irresponsible young

idiots who can't even be trusted to sit the right way on a toilet seat.

I close my eyes and wonder if I'll be able to interest anybody in bidding for the TV, newspaper, magazine, film and book rights to my story, and whether the proceeds will make up for the pocket money I'm about to lose.

One door closes, another opens.

Like Mr Bainbridge says, there's a world of opportunities out there.

ABOUT
THE AUTHORS

JACQUELINE HARVEY has spent much of her working life
teaching in girls' boarding schools. Her bestselling
Alice-Miranda series has been a runaway success in Australia
and has also been published internationally to great acclaim.
She is pleased to say that she has never yet encountered a
headmistress like her character, Miss Grimm, but she has
come across quite a few girls who remind her a little of
Alice-Miranda. Jacqueline has also published an increasingly
popular series for younger readers featuring an adorable
five-year-old girl called Clementine Rose, proud owner
of Lavender, a teacup pig. Visit Jacqueline's website at
www.jacquelineharvey.com.au

TRISTAN BANCKS is a writer and filmmaker. He has a
background as an actor and television presenter in Australia
and the UK. His short films have won a number of awards
and have screened widely at festivals and on TV. Tristan has
written a number of books for kids and teens, including the
Mac Slater, Coolhunter series, the My Life series (weird-
funny-gross short stories featuring Tom Weekly), *It's Yr Life*
with Tempany Deckert and *Two Wolves*. Tristan's drive is to
tell inspiring, fast-moving stories for young people. Visit
Tristan at www.tristanbancks.com

ALEESAH DARLISON writes picture books and novels for boys and girls of all ages. Her story themes include courage, understanding, anti-bullying, self-belief, friendship and teamwork. Aleesah's picture books are *Little Meerkat*, *Bearly There*, *Puggle's Problem* and *Warambi*. Her chapter books include *Fangs* and *Little Good Wolf*. Her novels and popular series are *I Dare You*, the Unicorn Riders series, the Totally Twins series and the Ash Rover series. When Aleesah isn't creating entertaining and enchanting stories for children, she's usually looking after her four energetic children and her frisky dog, Floyd. Her website is www.aleesahdarlison.com

COLIN THOMPSON was born in the UK and started writing and illustrating children's books in 1990. Since then he has had more than 70 books published. He has received numerous awards, including an Aurealis Award for the novel *How to Live Forever*, CBCA Picture Book of the Year for *The Short and Incredibly Happy Life of Riley* and CBCA Honour Book and the Family Therapists' Award for *The Big Little Book of Happy Sadness*. Colin has been shortlisted for many other awards, including the Astrid Lindgren Award – the most prestigious children's literature prize in the world. Colin lives in the beautiful town of Bellingen in NSW, where there is plenty of room for his dogs to enjoy life. His books for Random House Australia include numerous picture books, *How to Live Forever* and *The Second Forever*, the Floods series and the Dragons series. Visit Colin's website at www.colinthompson.com

Out shopping, **DIANNE BATES** is known as 'a granny grabber' because she always stops to talk to babies and toddlers. She loves chatting with older children, too. Di gets many story ideas from what students in her writing workshops tell her (like the boy who said that when he was three he super-glued his teeth together!). Di has published over 120 books for young readers. The most recent is *A Game of Keeps,* based on a girl who Di and her author husband, Bill Condon, fostered. Di and Bill live near Wollongong, NSW. Their website is www.enterprisingwords.com.au

GEORGE IVANOFF is an author and stay-at-home dad residing in Melbourne. He has written over 70 books for children and teenagers, and is best known for his You Choose interactive books and Gamers novels. He has books on both the Victorian and NSW Premier's Reading Challenge lists, and he has won a couple of awards that no one has heard of. George has also had stories published in numerous magazines and anthologies, including *Trust Me Too*, *Stories for Girls* and *Stories for Boys*. George drinks too much coffee, eats too much chocolate and watches too much *Doctor Who*. If you'd like to find out more about George and his writing, check out his website at www.georgeivanoff.com.au

JENNY BLACKFORD is a writer and poet interested in science fiction and fantasy, ancient history and religion, food, gardening and the natural world. She writes novels, stories and poems of all sorts of genres from serious to spooky for children, YA readers and adults. In 2001, she started writing full-time. Her historical novel *The Priestess and the Slave* was published in 2009, the year that she and her husband (and their ragdoll cat Felix) moved back home to Newcastle. In 2013 Jenny published an illustrated collection of cat poems called *The Duties of a Cat*. Visit Jenny's website at www.jennyblackford.com

KERRI LANE has been a full-time writer since 1995. She was a creative-writing tutor for Charles Sturt University's Enrichment Studies Program for eight years and tutored subjects via correspondence in creative writing and professional romance writing for the Australian College of Journalism. She has also spent three years as the National Vice-President of the Romance Writers of Australia, worked as a ghostwriter of non-fiction titles and judged many writing competitions. Kerri has written many books for young readers, including a number of titles in the Sprints series. Under the pseudonym of Kaz Delaney, she has published a number of YA novels including *Dead, Actually* and *Almost Dead*. Kerri lives at Lake Macquarie on the New South Wales central coast. Visit her website at www.kerrilane.com

MICHAEL PRYOR has published more than 25 fantasy books and numerous short stories, from literary fiction to science fiction to slapstick humour. He has been shortlisted at least six times for the Aurealis Awards, been nominated for a Ditmar award, and six of his books have been listed as Children's Book Council of Australia Notable Books. His series include the popular Chronicles of Krangor series for younger readers and his Laws of Magic and Extraordinaires series for older readers. *10 Futures* is a collection of interlinked stories in which Michael imagines what the next 100 years of human existence might be like. For more information about Michael and his books, please visit www.michaelpryor.com.au

ANDY GRIFFITHS is one of Australia's most popular children's authors. He is best known for the Treehouse series, his JUST! books and *The Day My Bum Went Psycho*. Over the last 20 years his books have been *New York Times* bestsellers, adapted for the stage and television and have won more than 50 Australian children's choice awards. Andy is such a passionate advocate for literacy that he's an ambassador for The Indigenous Literacy Foundation and The Pyjama Foundation. You can visit Andy at www.andygriffiths.com.au

ABOUT
THE EDITOR

Linsay Knight is widely respected as a leading expert in, and contributor to, children's literature in Australia. As former Head of Children's Books at Random House Australia, she nurtured the talent of numerous authors and illustrators to create some of Australia's most successful children's books. Linsay is also a lexicographer, having written and edited many dictionaries and thesauruses, is the author of a number of successful non-fiction books for children and adults, and the editor of a number of story collections, including *30 Australian Stories for Children*, *30 Australian Ghost Stories for Children* and two series of age-story collections like this one.

ABOUT
THE ILLUSTRATOR

Tom Jellett has illustrated a number of books for children, including *Australia at the Beach* by Max Fatchen, The Littlest Pirate series by Sherryl Clark for Penguin Books, *The Gobbledygook is Eating a Book* by Justine Clarke and Arthur Baysting, *My Dad Thinks He's Funny* by Katrina Germein and the follow up *My Dad Still Thinks He's Funny* for Walker Books. Tom has also been included in the Editorial and Book category for the Society of Illustrators Annual Exhibition, New York in 2013 and 2014. He was also included in Communication Arts Illustration Annual 2012, 3×3 Children's Show No. 9, 10 and 11, and was Highly Commended in the 2013 Illustrators Australia Awards. For more information about Tom and his work visit www.tomjellett.com

ACKNOWLEDGEMENTS

'Alice-Miranda and the Secrets of Sintra' by Jacqueline Harvey. Text copyright © Jacqueline Harvey 2014.

'Freak' from *My Life and Other Stuff That Went Wrong* by Tristan Bancks first published by Random House Australia in 2014. Text copyright © Tristan Bancks 2014.

'Zafarin's Challenge' by Aleesah Darlison first published in *The School Magazine* in April 2012. Text copyright © Aleesah Darlison 2012.

'The Haunted Budgie' from *The Haunted Suitcase and Other Stories* by Colin Thompson. First published by Hachette Children's Books in 1996. Text copyright © Colin Thompson 1996.

'Snake Man' by Dianne Bates first published by Random House Australia in 2014. Text copyright © Dianne Bates 2014.

'50 Cents' by George Ivanoff first published by Random House Australia in 2014. Text copyright © George Ivanoff 2014.

'Six Legs, Three Heads' by Jenny Blackford. First published in *The School Magazine* in February 2014. Text copyright © Jenny Blackford 2014.

'Pedro and the Perilous Paintbrush' by Kerri Lane first published by Random House Australia in 2014. Text copyright © Kerri Lane 2014.

LOOK OUT FOR THESE OTHER GREAT STORY COLLECTIONS

OUT NOW